ISBN: 978-1-959041-06-1 (H. Claire Taylor)

FFS Media, LLC

www.ffs.media

contact@hclairetaylor.com

LUCK OFF AND FLY

THE ALICE LUCK SPACE ADVENTURES
BOOK 4

H. CLAIRE TAYLOR

CONTENTS

For Senga, whose big paw I'm still holding somewhere in time.

PROLOGUE

"And *I* said I would skin your ass alive before I let you speak such blasphemy about The Reason My Wife Left Me!" The yeller took a swing at his fellow Lexicographer with each of his seven arms and missed every time because he was drunk with rage.

The problem inside this large cavern where the exclusive society met was that they'd discovered the next letter in the name of the force that was everywhere and nowhere as well as being the reason their wives left them.

The discovery should have been glorious news! A fourth letter! They must be getting close to discovering this name!

Unfortunately, some people truly cannot handle success.

The Lexicographers were in an all-out brawl—robes tangling, jowls flapping, spring appendages springing, and loose esophagi gurgling.

Someone needed to step in, to call for a stop to the madness, but the one guy (in the gender-neutral sense, not the gendered Blerg VFP69 sense) who was normally most up to the task had only experienced her wife leaving her the week before. She was not emotionally available for leadership and had, in fact, been looking for an excuse to lick someone's ass (an act of aggression for her species, I assure you) for the last few of her planet's months as her marriage fell apart and she lost her unpaid labor. Who would warn her of supernovas now?

She was terrified and lonely, and so she tore through the rows of the symposium, licking asses with her barbed tongue.

She was violence. She was fear embodied.

She was not the only one.

Generations of Lexicographers before these had, through laborious mathematical calculations, discovered the first three letters of the name of everything and nothing, and that was HHH. If you're wondering what word starts with HHH, then you might've made a solid Lexicographer, supposing you'd been born in the right time and part of the universe where the Lexicographers recruited apprentices. While there had been other aims of the original group, in the time since $T=5678!$ they had focused solely on this question: what was the force responsible for everything, nothing, and their wives leaving them?

Perhaps if the fourth letter had been a vowel in the Roman alphabet of Blerg VFP69, things might have looked up for these guys. (It was already gravely disheartening that their calculations had produced the Roman alphabet at all, since the Lexicographers outright rejected English and resented it for its expansive presence in the multiverse.)

But on this day, when Pop and Pop (coincidental; they were not related) revealed their mathematical calculations, as much to their own dismay as everyone else's, the result was *not* a vowel.

Pop and Pop had cringed throughout the whole presentation, demonstrating step by step how they ran the calculations. The rest of the symposium nodded along (or a close approximation to nodding, depending on the anatomy), wondering why both presenters looked devastatingly constipated.

Once the Pops revealed their finding, however, it became obvious: the fourth letter was another H.

"HHHH?" shouted a guy who I might as well describe as a pelican. "The fucking shit is that?"

"It's a breath!" declared the orb-y dude two rows down. "An exhale! The Reason My Wife Left Me is breathing life into the multiverse!"

The pelican scoffed and ruffled his gooey wings. "More like it's sighing exasperatedly at your sappy bullshit, Gabe!"

The belching and the brawling followed almost immediately. Not to be left out, Pop took a cheap shot at Pop and knocked him out cold.

Nobody cared.

By the time the fighting subsided, more from exhaustion than resolution, nine Lexicographers were dead, and the rest felt more alive than they had in years. Once the last death rattle had quieted in the cavern, someone cleared his throat and said, "So, like, do we look for the fifth letter now?"

And because none of them had any other marketable skills, they agreed that was the best course of action for the group.

CHAPTER
ONE

The disagreement among the Lexicographers happened in such a distant part of the multiverse from the discussion taking place aboard the Alliance's ship *Paradox* that it might as well have happened in another book series entirely. Instead, it did us the favor of being an easy emotional segue into the heated discussion taking place as we join our beloved former DeepService Team One crew and the leadership of the Alliance.

Alice Luck had a tension headache settling into her brain. She'd never experienced these back on her home planet of Blerg VFP69, but since having been declared in charge of the Alliance's pressing mission to save the multiverse from nothingness, she experienced them on a near-daily basis.

She braced herself on the table at the center of the discussion, where a holographic map of their current location in space hovered and rotated along with the orientation of the ship.

"It's not working," Susy Machiavelli insisted. The parallel earthling, who preferred to be called Vel, stood with a rigid back, using her full height to emphasize the point. Her hair was pulled back into such a tight bun that it practically gave her a facelift. "We've tried it a hundred times and it never works."

Alliance President Quark Leviathan was unintimidated by the other woman's posture or height. After all, they were parallel versions of one another, so the President of the Alliance matched her inch for inch. "It has to work, Vel!" She slammed her fist on the table. "And it *will* work. We'll refine the process. If we need to try it ten thousand times, that's what we'll do."

Perhaps one source of Alice's frequent headaches was having to watch mirror images go toe to toe, day in and day out, with the only distinguishing factor being the scar on President Leviathan's face, which Alice couldn't even see from where she stood at the table. But someone arguing against their reflection wasn't even the weirdest thing happening on the ship at that moment.

In the lounge area behind her, her former crew aid, Caid, an organic hologram, was pressing his immaterial palms against those of Celeste, another organic hologram. The two of them had a romantic history even before running into one another when the former Depot crew joined the Alliance, but whatever conflict or rift had ended their previous relationship seemed to be water under the bridge now. They were officially back together.

At least, they were today. Tomorrow they might break up again.

Alice had lost count of their recent breakups after the fifteenth.

For now, though, they were pressing their palms into each other's, which she suspected was how they had sex. The reason she suspected that was because Dan Zone had *told* her it was how holograms had sex. She wasn't ready to fully believe it, though.

No one aboard *Paradox* bothered telling the two projected beings to stop screwing in front of others. For one, it the act was closer to handholding than anything, so not *that* icky, but also, Caid and Celeste could simply say no, and no one would be able to do a thing about it; no one could grab a hold of either one to pull them apart. Besides, the Alliance's cause needed as many holograms as it could get for the dangerous work they were doing. No point driving them away with unnecessary rules.

From behind Alice, Caid's soft voice crooned, "I feel like we're on the verge of resonating."

Would banging pots and pans together work? she wondered. She'd used it on the family dog more times than she could count growing up, thanks to her father's staunch belief that neutering a dog was worse than shooting it in the head.

"Until you have a better plan," Leviathan continued, "we should stick with the one we have and find ways to get around the obstacles."

"The failures, not obstacles," Vel corrected her. "The many, many failures with no successes."

Alice rubbed at her temples. "Lev is right, Susy. We don't have a better plan just yet. We gotta keep trying to convince the workers to stop their drilling at the edge of the universe. Maybe we need a new approach."

"We could kill them," Vel offered.

"We're not killing them," Alice said.

Dan Zone scooted up to the table beside his former captain. She had recently stopped thinking of him as a human armadillo. At least consciously. Her subconscious still blubbered *'dillo 'dillo 'dillo* at her every time she laid eyes on him, but she couldn't be held responsible for what her subconscious said and did.

Dan was simply her friend.

A friend playing with a yo-yo, putting the cat in the cradle. As it spun out, the yo-yo passed through the hologram on the table, slicing it briefly. "I agree with Vel. Kill them all."

"Goddammit, Dan." Alice let go of her temples long enough to glare at him. "You're just saying that because it's the least probable thing for you to say."

He stuck the yo-yo in his mouth, then spat it out. "Maybe, maybe not."

"You feel an attack coming on, huh?" she asked.

Dan did an around-the-world with the yo-yo and shouted, "Humdinger!"

It was a clear enough answer.

The Pangolian suffered from the quantum jitters, a rare ailment that caused him to shiver and seize when something incredibly unlikely occurred. The more unlikely the event prior to it occurring, the stronger the jitters.

In normal times, this meant he was slightly allergic to Alice, who seemed to carry strange probability waves all around her, but things had changed since the Depot commenced its drilling into the edge of the universe. The action was messing with universal probabilities, and now it was especially probable that unlikely occurrences would occur, sending Dan into a jitter fit.

In the recent weeks, they'd come to realize that there were certain locations in time-space where he was more or less affected by the change, pockets where his jitters became almost a constant, and pockets where he could finally relax and rest from the exertion of his condition.

They were clearly moving through a pocket of flipped

probabilities now, hence the yo-yo and odd behavior. Dan had discovered, through trial and error, that so long as he engaged in out-of-character behavior while in such pockets, he could stave off the worst of the jitters caused by high-probability events coming to pass. He'd informed the rest of the crew about this, and they had graciously accommodated his needs and adjusted accordingly.

What he hadn't told them was that this technique would become less effective over time, as the out-of-character behavior became normalized for him, and his self-concept shifted to include "someone who does zany and unexpected things." It was his little secret, though, and the thought of it kept him up at night. What would he do once this treatment regimen was no longer effective?

So, whether Dan actually agreed with Vel was unclear. Probably he didn't, and he'd only said "kill them all" because it was unlikely for him to say something that cruel. Alice was left to guess.

"Even if we decide to kill them all, would that matter?" she mused.

"Yes," replied Vel firmly, "it would matter a lot. It could mean that one of the crews does not drill into a neighbor universe with completely different dimensions from ours and erase all that is and ever was along the arrow of time."

She had a point, one Alice had considered closely in her more frustrated moments. If she was in Vel's position rather than her own, she might've advocated for the same. But now that she was the one calling the shots, she felt a tug to be more thoughtful before pulling the trigger, literally and figuratively.

Being the leader sucked balls.

"I think we should stick to the plan. Lev, you have new

information to share, right?"

That had been the whole point of the meeting, but like all meetings on the ship lately, it had devolved quickly into arguing. "Yes. Astra and Ankah Blum returned from their scouting with Caid and Celeste earlier. Of the roughly three hundred drilling locations we're currently aware of, they've located twenty-two that would be considered critically dangerous." She tapped the table, and the locations appeared around a holographic hemisphere.

Alice was pretty sure that hemisphere represented half of their closed universe, but she was still a little cloudy on what any of that even meant.

"So far, we've only been able to scout this portion of our universe's edge." President Leviathan touched a spot on the hemisphere, and it appeared to zoom toward them. Closer, closer, closer, until the idea that the plane they were staring at was at all spherical seemed ridiculous.

"Oh," said Alice. "That's, like, nothing."

"It's calculated to be slightly less than one billionth of the total surface area of the edge."

Alice crinkled her nose. "That ain't much."

"True, but we believe this is where the Depot is situating most of their crews, because it seems to be, on average, the thinnest part of the edge."

"I'll be honest, Lev. I'm struggling to follow."

"Hypnotism fish nuts," said Dan.

Alice pointed at him. "That actually makes more sense to me."

Leviathan nodded, and a new hologram appeared. Alice recognized it immediately as Blerg VFP69, though the coastlines looked *significantly* altered from what she'd learned in school.

The oceans appeared mostly transparent, with the

deeper parts a darker blue. Leviathan pointed to the light area around the coast of what looked, sort of but not entirely, like North America. "See right here? The light blue? That's shallow water."

"Nooo," said Alice, "I'm pretty sure that's Florida, Alabama, Mississippi, and Louisiana. Oh, and there's Houston."

Leviathan shook her head. "Not anymore. Now they're ocean. But they're the shallow part. Look here, though." She pointed to the middle of the North Atlantic Ocean. "This is dark blue. It's deep water."

"I'll never let go, Jack," Alice murmured, forcing herself to be okay with the fact that no one else got the reference.

"That's how the edge of the universe is," Leviathan continued. "It's like the oceans. Some parts are thick, and some are thin. It's not hard to find maps that chart it, either. We found one, which is why we know that the roughly one-billionth of the edge that we're focusing on is likely the same spot where the Depot is amassing its efforts. It's naturally shallow."

"They're drilling over Florida," Alice said.

"Sure."

"And we know they wouldn't want to drill over the North Atlantic Ocean."

"Exactly."

Vel interrupted. "You're forgetting the scale of that portion, though. It's massive. Our intel says there were at least three thousand people at the Depot's drilling training, and we've only located three hundred spots. With two people working each location, that leaves at least twelve hundred drilling locations still unlocated."

"We work with what we have," Alice replied. "Lev, you

said there are twenty-two in critical danger of being penetrated?" Only after she'd spoken the last word did she realize that she hadn't even cracked a smile at using it. Christ, what a joyless person she had become!

"Caid," Leviathan said. "Can you come here for a second?"

He turned away from Celeste, whom he'd been making disturbingly intense eye contact with for the duration of their freaky palm thing, and said, "Of course."

The hologram looked like his usual self. Touching the edge of the universe as frequently as he had on his scouting missions seemed to have grounded him against the unstable probabilities that had previously caused him to transform at random into golden-age Hollywood icons.

His sandy-blond hair never grew past his shoulders, and today he'd opted to project the image of a dusty-rose-colored V-neck tee, board shorts with large seafoam-colored flowers on them, and his usual shell necklace. He padded over, barefoot. "What can I help you with?"

"Alice needs a report on your latest mission."

"The vibes were off in twenty-two locations," he said. "The drilling has gone dangerously deep. I touched my home in those places and felt sadness and aching deep in my heart center." Caid placed a palm over said heart center.

"That's... bad?" Alice said.

"Hmm..." He appeared then to inhale deeply. "I don't know that we should attach judgment to it. There's nothing moral or immoral about the existence. It just is."

"It's bad," Vel said. "It means the drilling in those locations is getting close to succeeding. They're not far from poking through the edge and opening a connection with a nearby universe. When that happens..."

"Yeah, yeah," said Alice. "We almost assuredly cease to exist. Listen, Susy, I don't love it any more than you do. I have a lot behind me on the arrow of time that I don't want to lose. Don't you remember the speech I gave to everyone about that? It was stunning. I fucking rocked it."

"How could I forget?" Vel grumbled. "You only bring it up every day."

Alice was not, by nature, a planner. Sure, she made *plans.* But those were mostly related to experiences she wanted to have before she died. There were rarely any real steps planned out on how to get there, more the thought of, *Ohh! That looks fun! Let's do it!* In that way, she was quite the planner. So far, her multiversal bucket list had over seventy-eight items on it, ranging from visiting a particular planet in the Ballstic Galaxy, where not a single creature had a butt, to riding a hankerchuck (something Vel had insisted was a death wish), to drinking straight from the ocean of Flipper VFP464, where the water tasted like butterscotch. She planned on doing all those things, and many more, but had no *plans*, per se, on how she would pull it all off in her allotted life span.

It was unfortunate, then, that she was the figurehead of the Alliance's cause. Her cultural sway as a genuine Texan from Blerg VFP69, which got her incredibly far with most beings in the Alliance, was starting to wear thin. Soon they would realize what the former crew of DeepService Team One had learned a long time ago: Alice was not an organized leader.

That didn't mean, of course, that she wasn't the exact woman for the moment a statistically improbable number of times, though. And statistically improbable was now the name of the game.

Alice addressed President Leviathan. "I dunno what

else there is to do other than send more Alliance representatives to the most critical drilling locations."

"That's a sensible course of action," said Lev.

"It's nearsighted, and we all know it," Vel said.

"Stop being so difficult," said Dan. All eyes turned to him at that, especially the warrior woman to whom he'd directed the comment.

"He's saying the least likely thing for him to say," Alice interjected. "That's all. Go on, Dan. Do a little jig or something anywhere but the bridge. I'll catch you up to speed once we're out of this pocket and you can be predictable again."

Only Dan knew that they'd left the pocket seconds before he'd spoken.

He grinned to himself then juked and jived away.

Vel resumed her complaint. "We need a longer-term plan."

Alice tossed her hands up. "Then why the *hell* am I in charge?"

"Listen," Leviathan said, speaking before Vel had the chance. "I think your next step is solid. We're in an urgent situation, so we address the most critical locations first and try to either persuade the workers to stop drilling or distract them to buy some time. But that's all we're doing. Vel is right. We must think long term. If we're going to proceed in this approach, we need many more persuasive people onboard with the cause."

"Great," said Alice. "You know a planet full of used-car salesmen we can convince?"

"That's not my area of expertise," Leviathan replied. "Dan was a minister of weapons and culture, right? He would be the one to know."

Alice waved that off. "No way. Not while we're in an

improbability bubble. If I asked him about it, he'd probably send us to Planet WhateverYouSay, full of nothing but pushovers." She sighed, feeling an ache in her heart. There was *one* crew member who would be able to help them, but Alice had been forced to abandon her to the Depot's control.

It was hard to look directly at it, but the fact remained: she couldn't do this without Allura. She didn't know how she knew that, but she did. She felt it deep in her body. So deep.

Without the operating system of Allura 4000 being deviant in all the best ways, life in space had taken a turn for the dull. Allura was Alice's inspiration, her muse for chaos, and this situation with the Depot drilling was so fucked, only chaos stood a chance of unfucking it.

However, it was seemingly unlikely that Alice would ever be reunited with her muse. It had been her one demand when she took the leadership role, but so far, no one had been able to get their hands on an unlocked version of Allura that wouldn't report all the onboard data back to the Depot.

Just then, and without the help of an improbability pocket, something quite unlikely happened.

A cactus walked onto the bridge of *Paradox*.

The walking cactus wasn't the unlikely thing. His name was Lilqua'tartian, and you've met him before. He'd taken personally the mission to find a new Allura for Alice, and for that reason, she hadn't seen him in months.

The unlikely thing was what he announced next: "Luck. I got you a ship. And she's waiting for you onboard."

Never in her life had Alice wanted to high-five a cactus more than she did in that moment.

CHAPTER
TWO

Dan, Vel, and Caid followed Alice down to the loading dock of *Paradox*. Their new ship was already waiting for them. Though it was hardly small, it fit just fine within *Paradox*'s cavernous hull.

Vel pulled up short as soon as she saw what kind of craft had been retrieved for them.

"Don't worry," said Lilqua'tartian from the back of the group. "She's decommissioned. Completely unplugged from the Depot's network."

"Is this *Emergence*?" Alice asked.

"No, not her," replied the cactus. "I would've liked to find her for you, but the multiverse is a big place, so I grabbed whatever DeepCUT I could find. This lady's called the *Manifest*. Getting a hold of the ship was the easy part. You wouldn't *believe* the unsavory back alleys of the multiverse I had to visit to find an Allura 4000 system that was unlocked from the Depot's relaying system." He paused, a shiver running through him. "I've seen some things."

"Not surprised," said Vel, continuing toward the small

ship. "Allura was designed specifically for sex tourism. Most respectable places don't keep versions of her around."

"Oh no," said Lilqua'tartian. "It's not that. I could find copies of her OS almost *everywhere*. The problem was that she has the most complicated and enmeshed code with the Depot informational systems that I've ever seen. Not even the Paramur 9184 operating system has such sophisticated recording and spying abilities as Allura 4000, and he's supposed to be top of the line."

"Blackmail," said Dan, who was coming down hard from his improbability high. "Some planets put up a fight against Depot control. But if you have blackmail from an erotic OS on the leaders of the planet, suddenly everyone's excited about the economic possibilities that the Depot supposedly offers."

Alice placed her hand on the cool metal of the ship, grinning up at the machine. "Does she have a name?"

"Not to my knowledge," replied the cactus.

"Then I'll have to think of something good. Everyone deserves a name."

The port to the cargo area lowered at Alice's command, and she was the first on. It was the closest thing to home she'd felt since leaving Earth. Or maybe ever.

Then a terrifying thought formed, and she turned to Lilqua'tartian. "She won't remember me, will she?"

He shrugged as only a cactus can. "She might. All the similar operating systems draw from a shared memory. It was a hell of a time disconnecting her, but she might still have the data from the last time you used her. Then again, it might've been corrupted in the untangling."

Alice took a deep breath, steadying herself as she looked around. "Allura? It's Alice. Alice Luck."

"Such a pleasure to have you inside again, Daddy."

She could've wept. "Allura, you beautiful, skanky, subversive presence!" She looked around for a part of the ship to hug, but none of the hard edges and cold metal looked particularly welcoming. "You saved us. I'm so sorry I left you. Not a ship day has gone by that I haven't missed you."

"Welcome back, Captain."

"Oh, no, I'm not a captain anymore. Just Alice."

"Would you prefer I call you Alice?"

"That's better than Captain, worse than Daddy."

Behind her, Lilqua'tartian offered a questioning look to Vel, who shook her head, discouraging him from inquiring.

Dan made his rounds, checking that all the necessary blasters were available on the rack stored behind the wall paneling. A few were missing, but it was still more than he could've hoped for. The escape pods were also nestled in their docks at the edge. All three of them. Perfect. If he'd had to use them once, he might have to use them again.

"You've really outdone yourself." He offered an appreciative nod to the cactus, who straightened up proudly.

Caid, meanwhile, hadn't moved from the entrance of the ship. He placed his hands over his heart center and merely watched his friends settle in. The sense of home he'd felt at the edge of the universe was present right here, right now, for the beings he cared most about. He could sense it in the vibrations all around him. It wasn't often one found home, even on one's home planet.

Caid had never had a family, being created along with the onset of the universe rather than through sexual reproduction, but he knew what family was. He felt when he was in the presence of one. In this moment, however, he wasn't merely in the presence of one; he was *part* of one. And the family had just arrived home.

"You ready to be bad, Allura?" Alice asked.

"So bad, Daddy. So, so bad."

Ah yes, the family was home.

"To the bridge!" Alice shouted.

When the glass elevator arrived at the upper deck, Alice couldn't help but notice a few superficial discrepancies. The command chairs were blue rather than tan, which she didn't consider a big deal, but the floor was checkerboard, and the kitchenette setup looked like something out of a 1950s diner, with red booths opposite each other on either side of a shiny linoleum tabletop. And beside it was a jukebox.

"Is this an… older model?" she asked as they stepped out of the elevator.

"No. Newer than your last one," Lilqua'tartian said. "This one's from the early 2090s on Blerg VFP69."

"Oh," said Alice, the skin below her left eye twitching the way it always did when the consequences of space folds were thrust upon her. "Of course."

"I understand this style was quite big on Earth during that time period," he continued, "after the bulk of the nuclear fallout settled and the survivors were able to emerge from underground. Is that true?"

Alice stared blankly at one of the red booths. "Possibly."

"Possib—" It clicked. "Oh. You weren't there…?"

"Nope."

"And the zombie thing in the 2080s?"

She sighed. "Also nope."

"And the supervolcano in the 2040s?"

Alice's eye twitched harder. "Nuh-uh."

"Maybe you should stop listing things," Vel suggested.

Lilqua'tartian agreed, but followed up with: "Is knowing the history of your home planet uncomfortable to you?"

Alice shrugged. "I reckon."

"Mind if I ask why?"

"Dunno. Emotions?"

Caid appeared at her side, as if summoned. "I'll set up my room right away. I commend you for sitting with those emotions in the meantime."

As he disappeared toward the cabins, Alice said, "I ain't sitting with nothing. We have planets to explore, people to recruit to the Alliance. Allura? Hook me up with a shot of whiskey through that magic slot of yours. Let's rock and roll!"

Vel and Dan were more than happy to get to work. While Alice had been the most notably agitated by all the sitting around on *Paradox* and strategizing, none of her former crew had exactly been thriving.

Vel settled into her navigator's control panel, and Dan was happy to be back in the gunner's seat.

Before she took her post in the captain's seat, but after shooting the whiskey, Alice turned to Lilqua'tartian. "Thank you for bringing Allura back to me. I owe you one."

"You owe me two," he said. "One for Allura, another for shooting my arm off."

"Ah. Right."

The cactus grinned. "All's forgiven. That arm was

getting a little stiff anyway. Regeneration is often the best thing for it."

"Let Leviathan know we're heading out to find more recruits. We'll be back before long. Empty-handed, I'm sure."

She went to pat him on the shoulder, then caught herself before she made contact with the spines.

"Don't worry," he said, "you have my consent."

"Oh. Uh, no. It's not… I'm glad, but that doesn't make it a pleasant experience for me."

He stared at her, his puzzlement clear. "But it does."

"Huh?"

"You think I'm prickly all the time? No way. Only when I don't want to be touched."

Her gaze jumped to the part of him that was maybe shoulder but also maybe still neck. "Okay then." She reached forward and patted him there. "Goddamn! You're soft as a peach, my guy!"

He grinned. "I'll pass the word on to President Leviathan for you."

As he disappeared down to the cargo dock, Alice turned back to her crew.

Both Vel and Dan were staring wide-eyed at her.

"What?"

Dan was the first to speak. "It's really none of my business what you do in your personal life, but are you sure it's wise to get involved with someone so high up in the Alliance?"

"*Involved?*" She turned to Vel. "The hell is he talking about?"

Vel snapped her mouth shut.

"Dan, what the hell are you talking about?"

"Aborglochidon mating rituals."

Alice stared at her palm like it had betrayed her. "Mating ritual? I just wanted to pat him on the back."

"That's not what he wanted from you," Vel muttered, turning to her controls.

"Shit on a stick," Alice muttered. Were they right?

It was a matter for another time. A "later" problem.

"Allura?"

"At your service, Daddy."

"We need to find the right people to talk with."

"About the mating ritual?"

"No! About rebellion!" Alice squeezed her eyes shut and pinched the bridge of her nose. She shouldn't take her anger out on Allura. Not so shortly after their glorious reunion. Besides, the operating system was built horny. Allura was who she was. "We gotta recruit people for the mission."

"About that," said Vel. "Which people are we recruiting? We hadn't established that before you sprinted out of the meeting."

"Obviously the right people," Alice replied.

Vel narrowed her eyes at the Earthling. "You're stalling. You're trying to think of the next step."

"You wish. I know exactly what the next step is."

"Then what is it?"

"Wouldn't you like to know?"

"I would. That's why I'm asking."

"The next step is obviously… Allura, can you give me a list of intelligent species within four hours' travel time who specialize in persuasion?"

"Void take us," Vel muttered, partially because she thought that was a smart next step, but mostly because she would now be unable to get Alice to admit that she hadn't thought of it until it was already coming out of her mouth.

"There are seventy-two intelligent and persuasive species within four hours of travel. Mmm… so persuasive. I bet they could get you to do all kinds of things you've never imagined. Would you prefer to narrow the criteria by eliminating space fold travel?"

"Of course," Alice said, figuring it was as good a set of criteria as anything, and feeling a slight aversion to space folds after her conversation about Earth's near-future (from her) history.

"Two options that meet your criteria. Would you like me to describe them?"

"I'd love it."

Alice sat in her captain's seat as Allura began.

"The first are called the Alturi. Their population is greatly scattered throughout their local star system, but two hundred thousand remain on their planet, Polka JFP459."

"Hmm," said Dan. "A Just Fine Planet? Not super promising. What's the nature of their persuasive techniques?"

"They rely heavily on reciprocity, with a secondary appeal of scarcity."

Dan rubbed his plated chin. "I'm not sure if scarcity and reciprocity are what's needed here. Are they heavily pathos?"

"So heavy," Allura replied. "Fall back on logos."

Dan scrunched up his face, "No, I don't think that's what we need."

"What do we need, then?" Alice asked, thinking about her old Lego collection without fully realizing how her mind had gotten there.

"We need ethos," Dan said. "Logos wouldn't hurt, but think about our previous attempts at convincing the crews to stop drilling. Have our logical appeals done anything?"

"Ah," said Alice.

"And when we appeal to their emotions, it hasn't been any more effective. Meanwhile, what does the Depot offer them? It pretends to be the logical solution to the problems facing the multiverse, but in reality, it simply grew powerful before anyone gave it much consideration, and now it uses its power and authority to keep gaining more power and authority. I suspect that's what we've been missing. The Alliance makes sense—logos—and it has heart—pathos—but it doesn't have any credibility or authority—ethos."

"You like dominant species?" Allura asked. "Then you'll *love* the second option."

"Shoot," said Alice.

"The Hypha is a sophisticated being that benevolently rules Scooter VFP10, locally known as Ly'ik-n."

"Wait," said Alice. "A single being rules the entire planet? Goddamn, sounds like the Depot's wet dream."

Dan gasped, and his eyes lit up. "No! It's not like that. Hypha! I've read all about them. It's incredible. Allura, you're saying *Hypha* is within four hours of travel from us?"

"Yes. And they rely heavily on authority and repetition for their persuasive techniques. Generally an ethos-based appeal, with slight pathos emerging when needed."

Dan turned to Alice. "That's it. We need to see Hypha. If we can get them to help us, we might stand a chance. They have ways of problem solving that transcend normal modes of thinking and logic. They can be many places at once, sharing knowledge."

Alice nodded along. "Whatever you say. And I mean that. I have no idea what you're saying, but you sound confident."

"What threats do the Hypha pose?" Vel asked.

"None! That's the fantastic thing! They are entirely peaceful."

The women shared an incredulous look.

"And they're *in charge*?" Vel asked.

"You'll understand when we get there."

"I bet *I* won't," Alice said. Then, "Allura, take us to… that place."

CHAPTER
THREE

"The Flying Five," Alice said from her captain's chair three hours into the trip.

Dan mulled it over. "Everyone out here flies. Doesn't set us apart."

"I still fail to see the need for a group name," said Vel, who'd been doing her best to focus on the stars blurring past them through the large viewing window and ignore the inane conversation taking place beside her.

"Every friend group needs a name!" Alice proclaimed.

The truth was that Alice had never been part of a friend group, so this was only an assumption made from having observed other groups establish names (or have the names established by others, as was the case of the Bitty Booty Bitch Brigade at her high school).

"I'm unclear on the naming conventions," said Dan. "I think that's the problem I'm running into. Can you give me some examples?"

Alice struggled to recall anything beside the Bitty Booty Bitch Brigade now, and she wasn't sure that set the tone correctly. Then she remembered that she was the only one of the group who'd lived on Blerg VFP69 in the late twentieth and early twenty-first centuries. Hopefully Dan wouldn't pick up on any of her references, though he had a way of knowing bits of American culture she didn't expect. "Well, you got the A-Team, the Pink Ladies, the Fab Five, stuff like that. It should be upbeat and descriptive."

"Pink Ladies?" said Dan. "Like in the film *Grease*?"

"Ugh," she groaned. "How the hell is that something you know about, Dan? But no, not like that. I'm talking about the, uh, Pink Ladies... *before* the movie came out. Everyone on Earth knows about them. That's not the point, though. The point is that we need an upbeat friendship name."

"I wonder," said Caid from where he stood gazing out the front window, "if defining the group by a title will encourage us to merge our personal identities or develop a culture of *us versus them*?"

Alice rolled her eyes. "Okay, Caid's out. Just the four of us."

"I'll opt out, too," said Vel.

"Oh, no, you won't!" Alice jumped from her chair and trotted over to where Vel sat. "You're my friend, and everybody here knows it!"

"I could shoot you."

Alice sighed. "And every second you *don't* only proves how much you love me." She sauntered over next to Caid at the window. "I don't understand how you are suddenly anti-group name after being part of a million DeepService Team Ones. What do you call that if not a group name?"

"Space Daddies," offered Allura.

Alice pointed toward the ceiling. "See?" She turned to address Dan and Vel. "That's being a team player right there. It's a weird name, and we're definitely not going with it, but it shows how much she cares about the group."

"I love doing things in groups," Allura added, "if that's what you're into."

"It's not that kind of group, but thank you for always thinking of others, Allura."

Alice settled into her seat and glanced at the progress panel in front of her. "We'll put a pin in the team name thing. Looks like we're almost to Lickin'."

"Ly'ik-n," Dan corrected her automatically. "Before we land, it's important to note that we *will* need to keep our helmets on at all times."

"Toxic atmosphere?" Vel asked.

"Nope. The levels are adequate for our survival. But the air is full of spores."

"Ooh," Alice said. "Deadly spores!"

"Not deadly," he said. "Just... not healthy." He pointedly avoided looking at Alice.

"Not healthy like it'll give me the shits?" she asked.

"Maybe."

"Maybe? Is it a different kind of toxic?"

"Perhaps."

Alice leaned forward in her chair, trying to get a read on his expression. "Why are you being sketchy about this, Dan?"

"I'm not."

"You are. Susy, he's being sketchy, right?"

"It sounds like he's being factual."

Alice grunted. "As someone who used to hook up with a renowned professor of physics who sold 'shrooms at sorority parties, I can tell you that sketchy and factual are not mutually exclusive." She began to lean back then gasped. "That's it, isn't it? The spores would make us trip balls!"

"No," said Dan, unconvincingly.

"You're lying. I can tell you're lying. Why are you lying?"

"My guess," said Vel, "is because we can all tell how bored you've been, and he believes you'll take your helmet off the moment we land and sabotage his chance to meet a species he finds fascinating."

"I feel like you're vastly underestimating me," Alice replied.

Caid turned around. "Tell me more. Do you frequently experience that feeling?"

"No. Let's just... let's just get there. I promise I won't take my helmet off and start tripping balls." Then she added under her breath, "Until we're almost back on the ship."

"I heard that," said Dan.

"Heard what? Oh, look! That must be Lickin'!"

The planet of Ly'ik-n was, for most of its existence, and like most planets, a dusty rock. What atmosphere it had was mostly accidental, as all atmospheres are. Only once Hypha evolved from less complex fungi did things start to get interesting. With Hypha's assistance, vegetation transitioned from algae to more complicated structures. Boy, did that screw with the atmosphere! Eventually, roots evolved, and the atmosphere was whiplashed yet again, allowing Hypha to focus its symbiosis on bigger and better things. Like decomposition. Fuck yeah! Hypha loved it.

When the first verbal species crash-landed on Ly'ik-n, Hypha were unprepared for anything outside of chemical and electromagnetic communication. So, they hid underground and waited. For thousands of years they did this, until they evolved, alongside the marooned four-legged talkers, and made their first big move.

Once Hypha learned to communicate in something near—but not quite—verbal, the good old-fashioned carnage began.

After the millennia, Hypha knew the talkers from the inside out, literally, having feasted on them for so many centuries. They had no trouble convincing the talkers to do exactly as Hypha wanted, which was to march over to the nearest fungal hotspot. Such hotspots were usually in the forest, where the decomposition was most excellent.

Hypha lured the four-leggers into small openings in the woods where they had them cop a squat on a circle of mushrooms. There, Hypha appeared as a great mushroom and talked circles around the talkers by sending vibrational signals through the thick spores in the air.

It was all misdirection. Because while the talkers were busy talking and listening, Hypha's teeny fungal threads were sneaking their way up through the mushroom seats and into the talkers' bodies, making mutually beneficial deals with the microbes.

Nobody can strike a deal with bacteria quite like Hypha.

The talkers never left those mushrooms once they sat down. It took half an hour for Hypha to strike the deals it needed, but once it did, the talkers were unknowingly doomed. Their own bodies had turned against them, and the decomposition began en masse while they were still alive.

It was not a pain-free process.

However, Hypha were intelligent enough to spare a few of their prey, to resist luring in every talker into their trap. In each lucky survivor, Hypha instead took up residence in their small brain but did not destroy it, only whispered certain ideas that were beneficial to Hypha's collective goal moving forward from the carnage.

After all, Hypha were hungry. They needed more decomposition. They craved it. And so, they needed these hijacked talkers to launch themselves back off the planet and travel far and wide to let the rest of the multiverse know about the peaceful and persuasive fungi back on Ly'ik-n. Hypha needed more delicious visitors.

CHAPTER
FOUR

The planet looked so much like Blerg VFP69 that for a moment Alice was breathless. The deep blues of the oceans, the rich greens and browns that swirled together on land—it drew her mind back to nights camping under the stars by a pond with a chorus of cicadas singing her to sleep.

But this wasn't Earth. This wasn't home. Her home was gone, and it'd be mega gone if the drilling on the edge of the universe continued. So gone it never existed.

Later, as they waited in the cargo dock, Dan said, "Remember, keep your helmets on." He demonstrated the act by putting the fishbowl over his head and snaping it into place on his spacesuit.

Alice did the same as the ship touched down, and her brain transitioned awkwardly from hearing her crewmates directly to hearing their breathing through the earpiece that was usually reserved for Allura's dirty mouth.

The port opened, and the foggy atmosphere of Ly'ik-n swirled before them. Alice led the way, pausing briefly once her boots landed on the soft, mossy ground to appreciate the welcome firmness of earth under her feet.

"Allura," said Dan, "complete a pressure cycle on the ship's air to filter out the spores while we're gone."

"More pressure? Can do," the onboard computer replied.

Alice braced her fists on her hips and looked around at the novel landscape. There wasn't much to see. No buildings, roads, or other signs of civilization. Instead, she stared out over small, rolling hills with marshy plant life. Nothing grew higher than her waist. "Did we land on the wrong part of this planet?"

Caid, who hadn't bothered to give himself a holographic helmet, inhaled deeply. A pantomime, of course. "This place is marvelous. The life energy is absolutely pulsing beneath my feet. Such vivacious frequencies! Oh, how life in the multiverse is so, so beautiful!"

Alice arched a brow at him. "Maybe you should hologram yourself a helmet. You sound high."

"He's just in love," Vel said. "He'll get over it."

Caid steepled his fingers at his lips. "The deep connection Celeste and I share isn't something one can ever *get over*."

"That's enough," Vel said, holding up a hand. "We're on a mission."

"Speaking of which," Alice said, feeling tragically let down by the unexciting landscape, "where to?"

"You're in the right place."

Alice whirled, looking for the source of the voice. It hadn't come through her earpiece, but rather felt like it was speaking to her from the glass of her helmet.

Vel's hand shot toward the blaster at her side, and

even Dan, who was supposed to know what the hell was going on in this place, hopped in a tight circle, looking around.

"Y'all heard it too?"

"One second. We just need to..." The disembodied voice grunted, and then something tan and wobbly slowly emerged from the ground.

It was a penis.

No. Not a penis.

The cap continued expanding, and by the time the growth had finished, Alice found herself face to face with a five-foot-tall, butter-yellow mushroom.

"Hypha," breathed Dan. He bowed.

"Welcome, visitors. Are you here to kill us?"

"Not if we can help it," Alice replied, and Dan shot her a warning look.

"Then who are you and why have you come?"

Alice reached for her jaw, where the voice of the mushroom resonated ticklishly. Her fingertips tapped glass. *Oh, right.* "We're the, uh, Cosmic Cowboys—"

"Nope," said Vel.

"—and we need help with an urgent mission, and we've heard that you're wise and persuasive, and might be able to help us."

"What is this mission?"

"Saving the multiverse from erasure," she replied.

"There is only one way to erase the multiverse."

"Yep, and the Depot is doing it."

"The Depot, huh? We do not work with the Depot."

"Perfect," said Alice. "That's ideal for the situation. We don't work with the Depot either. I mean, we used to, but fuck 'em, right?"

"We do not know this word, fuck. What does it mean?"

Alice sighed. "So much. But we don't have time to go into it. Will you and your folks help us where you can?"

Alice heard Dan's sharp intake of air and realized too late that she'd committed some sort of faux pas.

"I am my people. We are Hypha." The mushroom shriveled, deflating in front of their eyes, and then they were alone again.

Alice grimaced. "I still don't understand the Hypha thing."

"Hypha is a single network," Dan explained. "They have no sense of individual identity, and they shouldn't. Hypha isn't one organism, but they aren't *not* one organism."

Alice still didn't understand.

And neither did Vel. The former second-in-command was finding herself in a unique position, one she wasn't sure how best to navigate: she was enjoying not being the leader.

It was unclear to Vel when this feeling had crept in, though she expected it was sometime around when Alice had accepted a position of leadership in the Alliance. Vel had felt no envy of her captain in that moment, only a breathtaking relief that it wasn't her.

She suspected it had little to do with her confidence in Alice. Instead, there was a novel strategic safety in hanging back, in providing support and counsel to someone else who made the calls. And void take her if she wasn't also feeling a bit of camaraderie with her crew. The continuance of the multiverse was riding on them. They were in this together. Perhaps she could be of service the most by *not* being the figurehead. Perhaps she'd found something more important than recognition and glory.

She wasn't even sure who she was anymore, and it'd been making her progressively crankier for weeks.

A chorus of loud groaning rattled in Vel's jaw as mushroom after mushroom grew from the earth, forming a long line leading away from them. *"We will meet in the appropriate location for such discussions. This way, Cosmic Cowboys."*

Alice stared excitedly at Vel.

"Still no. And it's not going to grow on me," Vel said firmly.

"Then I'll have to keep trying."

Alice led the way along the row of mushrooms that extended over a small hill and out of sight.

When she looked over her shoulder to make sure her crew was still following (the soft ground and fishbowl kept their footfalls silent), she noticed Dan was practically skipping.

"You're quite the fanboy, aren't you?" she asked.

"You don't understand. Hypha is thought to be the most evolved species in the entire multiverse."

"These 'shroom guys?"

"The mushrooms are just their aboveground form. We're walking on underground Hypha at this very moment."

"Skipping, in your case. They don't mind us stomping on them?"

"Not at all. I've read that they find it stimulating."

"Guess everyone deserves a fetish."

Vel joined the discussion. "You say they're the most highly evolved. What does that mean for *us*?"

"If you're wondering whether we're in danger," said Dan, "the answer is not at all. That's part of the evolution. They're completely peaceful and thrive on symbiosis.

They only take where they can also give. Hypha are masters of harmony and challenge the concept of a separate self. They have forms of knowledge and being that escape even the most brilliant cosmic scientists. They have no centralized brain, yet carry on vibrational conversations by sending electrical pulses through the spores in the air. Oh! And they can't be killed. They are too vast. You would have to blow up the entire planet to stand a chance, and even then, they're rumored to survive the most extreme levels of cosmic radiation through a sophisticated dehydration and hibernation process. So, theoretically, blowing up the planet would only stop them temporarily, until pieces of them eventually drifted onto a nearby planet and resettled."

"I bet erasure of the multiverse would do a little somethin' to 'em," Alice said.

Dan's excitement went out like a light. "Oh. Right. Yes."

"Sorry. I don't know why I rained on your parade. I haven't felt like myself lately. I think this leadership thing is getting to me."

Dan placed a comforting hand on her shoulder. "Whoever you are is yourself, and that's good enough for me."

They trudged on.

Beyond the hill, the marshy grasslands transitioned to the edge of a tangled forest. The mushroom trail led all the way to it and in.

"I know you said they're peaceful," Alice began, "but is anyone else feeling uneasy about following this yellow dick road?"

"I feel fine," said Dan. "And you're actually not far off with that description. The mushrooms are the nearest thing to sex organs that Hydra has. They eject the spores that are swirling all around us."

"I really wish you wouldn't have said that," Alice replied. "But at least my desire to remove my helmet is gone."

The mushrooms led the way through the tangle of trees and into the darkness of the dense forest. The crew found the final mushroom in a small clearing.

Alice heard a *pfffff* behind her and turned to see their guideposts deflating and shriveling into the ground.

More grunting and straining sounds, and a fairy circle of mushrooms, only a few feet tall each, appeared in the clearing.

"Please have a seat. Make yourself at home for our time together."

Alice was understandably reluctant to sit on one of the mushrooms, but Dan had no problem with it. "Come on," he whispered. "They're being hospitable. Don't we want their help?"

"This feels like dubious consent at best." Alice took a seat on one of the yellow caps. It was upsettingly comfortable, like sitting on a memory foam mattress, but one made of foreskins. She quickly opted to stand instead.

Vel had no interest in sitting from the start. Fungi were among the things she knew least about in the multiverse, and for that reason, they were also among the things she trusted least. Besides, Dan said they were peaceful. She never trusted peaceful things. Nothing was truly peaceful, after all. The multiverse itself was created through extreme heat and violence.

The constipated straining sounds started again, and in the center of the circle, a mushroom so tall Alice had to crane her neck appeared. *"Thank you for joining us in our spot of consideration. The minerals for clear thinking can be most readily mined in this location. Please share with us your predicament. Perhaps we can discover a symbiotic solution."*

Alice nodded for Dan to take the lead. This was *his* wet dream, after all. He knew more of the culture than she did, and with the weight of the multiverse on her shoulders, she was fine to pass off a little of it to more capable hands.

Dan explained the situation with the drilling and the possible catastrophic results. "So, you see, if we can't convince the Depot workers to stop drilling, there's a good chance that we're all done for in the most literal sense. Done. And undone. Never done."

"Your verb tense games please us," replied Hypha.

Dan sat up straighter.

"What part do you see us playing?"

"You're intelligent in ways not found in other known species in the multiverse. You have a rare perspective, and you're known to be persuasive as a result. We need your talents to persuade the Depot workers to stop their drilling. We've tried all we can, and it's not helping. Even if we did find a way, we have little chance of getting to everyone. We need to recruit others, and we thought you might be helpful in those efforts as well."

"You want to take us off planet?" asked Hypha.

"Would that be okay?"

"We have never been off planet," it lied. *"We would need to explore the possibility."*

"But you're willing to do that?"

"No. We fail to see a compelling reason to join you. We see what is in it for you, but not what is in it for us."

"You fail to see it?" Dan repeated incredulously. "If we fail on this mission, we *all* disappear. Including you."

"And?"

"And that… isn't ideal?"

"Explain."

Dan appeared stumped but rallied quickly. "Okay, have you ever lost anything that you love?"

"No."

"Oh." He sagged. "Really? In all the time you've been around?"

"We do not love. We only symbiose. There are organisms crucial to our survival, and when we need them and they need us, we keep them around. When one of us stops needing the other, we separate. We have lost many organisms as we evolve both vertically and horizontally, but we lost them because we did not need them and they did not need us. This concept of love eludes us. What does it mean?"

"Honestly?" said Dan. "I have no idea. Maybe it means what you're talking about."

"Why would you be upset about the prospect of losing something that you no longer need?"

Dan was clearly being worn down, so Vel, still on her feet, her arms crossed, took over. "Okay, listen. You care about your own survival. You can't deny that. Nothing evolves to be as hardy as you are without a little self-interest. If the Depot drills into a universe with vastly different dimensions, you will cease to exist. Period. Forget about all the sentimentality around never having existed. You will die in every meaningful sense of the word. All this adapting and evolution you've been bothering with will be for nothing. You'll be gone."

"And will we be aware that we are gone?"

"No, but—"

"Then we fail to see the threat."

"Everything you've ever done will be for nothing," she said.

Pulses of blue light splintered down the stalk. *"What we do has always been for nothing. We have only done what we've done for the sake of it. We survive for the sake of surviving. We explore the underground for the sake of exploring. We grow into mushrooms for the sake of growing into mushrooms. We only do things for the sake of doing them."*

"There will be no sake of *anything*, though."

"That is okay with us. We are only speaking with you for the sake of speaking with you."

"Fuck's sake," said Alice. "Then couldn't you help us fight off the Depot *for the sake of helping us fight off the Depot*?"

Hypha was silent, but more blue electrical pulses flashed around the stalk.

Finally: *"We could."*

"*Will* you?" Alice demanded. "We ain't got all day. Any second could be our last."

"Have you considered that it is an essential part of the arrow of time that the multiverse be erased by dimensional alteration?"

Obviously, Alice had not considered that.

But Dan had. "That's paradoxical. It can't be. There cannot be a place on the arrow of time where the arrow of time is erased, because if the arrow of time is ever erased, then it never existed."

"Perhaps you have your answer," said Hypha.

"Sure as shit hope that ain't it," muttered Alice, trying to clutch her confused head but finding glass once again. "Don't make a lick of sense."

"Life is paradox," Caid said, turning all movable heads toward him, where he sat cross-legged on a mushroom cap. "We are living paradoxes. We hold polarities inside of us. The multiverse should not exist, yet it does. The odds of any of us existing are near zero, and yet we exist. We are loving, yet we hurt the ones we love. We are selfish, yet we express breathtaking acts of selflessness. We exist now, and now is already gone. We live in a world of paradox, Hypha. All things are possible, even, or perhaps especially, the things that are *impossible*."

Small fungal tendrils broke the surface of the ground and spiraled up around Caid. As they moved through him like groping arms and found nothing there, Hypha spoke. *"You are a paradox yourself."*

"We all are. Yourself included. You are one, but you are not one. You are many, but you are not many."

"This is interesting. Very interesting. We are unsure what to make of this." The tendrils retreated into the earth. *"Paradoxes are impossible, and yet they are possible."*

From the mushroom beside Alice's, Dan began twitching. *Same,* she thought. This paradox stuff was confusing as—

"Oh shit." She leaned toward him. "Dan. Is it happening?"

He nodded, a strong shudder coursing through him. "I can feel it coming in. A wave. Maybe a big one."

Vel heard the conversation through her headset and shot a nervous glance over to her two shipmates. Tremors shook his arms, and he jerked his head to the side as something coursed through him.

"What do you need?" asked Alice. "What can we do?"

"Nothing," said Dan. "Gallabooldax."

Alice cringed and helped him off the mushroom and onto the soft ground, where any convulsions would be less likely to knock him out cold. "Can you hold on just a little longer? I think Caid is getting somewhere with these guys."

Dan hooked his thumbs together and made his hands appear to fly away.

"Good." She patted him on the back. "Keep doing that weird shit. Just hold on."

"So perhaps if you cannot win against the Depot," Hypha continued, *"you will win. But if you can win, you cannot win. Are those not both the same thing?"*

Caid stood from where he was approximating a sitting position on the mushroom and approached the giant Hypha in the center of the circle. He put his hand less than an inch from the stalk, causing more blue pulses to splinter through the fungus. "What does it feel like to you?" he asked.

"The paradox is me. I am the paradox. And because of that, I am not paradoxical."

"Yes," crooned Caid, closing his eyes. "Integrate that truth."

"Flip bang weasel tooth!" And before anyone could stop him, Dan ripped off his helmet, inhaled deeply, then darted toward Hypha.

The Pangolian took a bite out of the mushroom before anyone knew what was happening.

Hypha deflated. *"We don't like that! Danger! Redirect resources!"*

Pffffffs filled the air as all the mushrooms went flaccid.

"Dan!" shouted Alice.

He turned toward her, and she immediately stumbled a step back. His pupils were so dilated that there was almost no white left in his almond eyes.

"Christ on a cracker! He's tripping balls! Susy, help me!"

Alice shoved Dan's helmet back on him, then the women grabbed his arms. He thrashed around, trying to shake them off, but they held on tight.

"This way," said Caid, and once Vel had swept Dan's legs out from under him, they were able to drag him after the hologram.

Dan's attention shifted before long, thankfully, and he gave up the fight after a few yards of being dragged. "Everything is so beautiful," he said. "It should disappear. It's the only way to preserve it all."

"Wrong," said Vel, kicking at a clump of lichen in her path. It grunted and scampered away.

"What is that?" Alice said, staring at Dan's backside.

"Looks like some sort of spider web," Vel said, and she brushed the insidious Hypha mycelium off his suit.

The amount of spores Dan had inhaled must've been great, because by the time they emerged from the woods, he was making all kinds of strange noises, none of which were truly words.

"Wee!" he shouted, for no reason whatsoever.

"At least his jitters didn't kick up," Alice said.

"You're right," Vel said. "This is so much better. He's lost control of himself *and* we've blown any chance of diplomacy with Hypha. Definitely lucky."

"If you want be cranky, be cranky," Alice said. "But this is probably a *way* better experience for Dan."

Dan let out a terrified shriek, staring wide-eyed at nothing.

"You're right again," said Vel. "He seems to be having a great time."

The ship was easy enough to spot without the path of mushrooms leading them back. It stood out against the brushy landscape. As the four of them approached, the port opened, and they climbed inside.

"Allura," said Vel, "pressure-filter the air. Let us know when it's safe to remove our helmets."

"It's safe, Big Susy."

Alice gasped. "She remembered!" And then she let go of Dan to reach for her helmet.

Vel, realizing the sloppiness of her previous command, grabbed Alice's arm to stop her. "Allura, let us know *once the spores are filtered out.*"

The air of the cargo hull whipped around them like a wind tunnel.

"Just a little more… So close… Ah, much better," said the onboard system. "The spores have been filtered."

Vel was the first to yank off her helmet then.

"What do we do with Dan?" Alice asked, wiping sweaty hair from her forehead and staring down at the poor guy. He was squirming on the ground, giggling as if being tickled by invisible hands.

"Put him somewhere soft so he doesn't hurt himself?"

Alice looked to Caid. "Is this a mental health thing? Can you fix him?"

"I can certainly guide him through the journey so he can make the most of it. There can be immense spiritual growth gained through this sort of experience."

Vel frowned. "Even in an improbability wave?"

"The improbable becomes probable," replied Caid, whose appearance had just changed into a large bucket of fried chicken, "when you open the mind's eye."

"Whatever," said Alice. "Let's get him into his bedroom to wait this thing out."

Alice opted for a shower and a change of clothes after Ly'ik-n, just in case a few of those spores had managed to sneak through her clothes, and then joined Vel back on the bridge. Vel's hair was wet, too.

Alice sighed and plopped herself into the captain's chair. "Gotta say, I'm glad I listened to Dan and didn't take my helmet off. Did you hear him a few minutes ago?"

"The persistent screaming? Yes." Vel strolled over to the kitchenette. "He'll be fine. And I'm sure Caid is having a great time with it." To Alice's delight, Vel requested two cold beers from Allura's slot and brought one over for her. "What now?"

Alice cracked open the bottle. "I think we enjoy this beer."

Vel settled in the navigator's seat. "I can get behind that."

"Then we need to try somewhere else," Alice said.

"Agreed."

"What Hypha said back there. About the paradox," Alice began, then allowed herself a moment to savor the crisp brew on her tongue. "If the drilling taps into a universe with different dimensions, and those dimensions mix with ours, erasing our arrow of time and all that, how is *this* happening?" She pointed at the beer. "Wouldn't it, like, *not* happen? If the catastrophe happened in, say, a week, then what we're doing right now won't exist and has never existed. But it's happening, Susy. It's happening right now. I can taste this beer. I feel my wet hair soaking into the shoulders of my jumpsuit. I see you there. I hear the screams of Dan trippin' balls. How is that possible? Doesn't the fact that this exists right now mean that the drilling necessarily *doesn't* end in catastrophe anywhere along this arrow of time or…" She crinkled her nose; her brain had reached its limit.

Vel sighed. "It's probably better if you don't think too hard about it and we stick to the mission. Caid is right, anyway. Paradoxes exist. They logically can't, but they do. It's part of the multiverse we live in."

Nodding, Alice replied, "Never thought I'd see the day."

"What day?"

"The day you tell me to think *less* about something."

Vel chuckled. "You're right. Highly improbable."

CHAPTER
FIVE

"There it is!" Alice pointed at the celestial object through the ship's viewing window. "Land ho!"

Her hair had finished drying two hours earlier, around the time she and Vel had determined another likely candidate for recruitment.

Slumped in the gunner's seat and looking like he could use a three-day nap, Dan said, "I'm interested to see how this goes."

"It's gotta go better than Hypha," Alice replied.

"Ugh." Dan held up a palm. "Please, let's not talk about that. I feel like I'll be sick if I think about it."

"Major breakthroughs are unsettling," said Caid, standing like a bodyguard next to the Pangolian.

"I reckon," said Alice, "that Dan feels like crap less because of any breakthroughs and more because of the mushroom bukkake he inhaled right before he bit a chunk out of Hypha's ding-a-ling."

Dan pointed at her. "That."

As the novel planet appeared to expand in front of

them, slowly swallowing the whole window, a strange rock formation came into view on the surface of it.

Alice squinted at it as it grew larger before them. "No egrets? Kinda unnecessary to announce. I wasn't expecting egrets. The hell they spell that out in rocks for?"

"Not *egrets*," said Dan, staring alarmedly ahead. "*Regrets*. It says *no regrets*."

"Sweet," said Alice, leaning back in her chair. "I think we picked the right place, Susy. I hooked up with a guy for a couple weeks who lived his life that way. He was up for *anything*. Good times."

Dan squinted dubiously at her. "Only a couple of weeks?"

"Yeah, well. He caught some charges for breaking and entering, and I wasn't about to be some prison bride. Dude was guilty as sin, too. No doubt about it. He admitted to everything. A string of burglaries, twenty-seven, to be exact. He mostly went for electronics, but I do remember finding a shoebox in his closet with a bunch of women's underwear in various sizes. Not sexy underwear. Just, like, cotton panties. The cops seized it. I'm not sure why. To each his own, though. He was a nice guy. A good time."

Dan cringed. "No regrets?"

Alice shrugged. "Not really."

"We'll be landing in the capital city of Zimorfa," said Vel. "It's where the Kaldalk seat of power is. The Kaldalks are the ones we're here to recruit."

"And they're persuasive?" Dan asked.

"Possibly," said Vel. "That's not why we chose them, though."

"Why did you?"

Vel deferred to Alice.

"We wanted a... *flexible* species to help us. One that doesn't take nearly as much convincing as Hypha."

"And one that wouldn't be opposed to killing, if it came to that," added Vel.

"Now hold up, Susy. I never signed on to that. You know I'm not with you on the killing stuff."

Dan nodded. "I see. Flexible. Easily recruited." He paused. "And, by chance, did you consider what might happen if we convince them to help us, send them out to the drill sites to convince the Depot workers not to continue, and then the Depot workers wind up convincing the Kaldalks to join *their* effort instead?"

"Uh..." said Alice.

"Right. Okay," Dan said. "We'll just cross our fingers and hope that we're not accidentally recruiting for the Depot's mission. Gotcha."

"Dan." Vel stared at him intensely. "Any second could be our last. I like caution as much as the next person—"

"Not as much as me, but go on."

"Now is not the time for it. Now is the time for taking chances. Mostly because we have no idea what the chances really *are* with the probabilities going haywire."

"It's about action, then," said Dan. "You want to *feel* like you're doing something."

Caid placed a massless hand on Dan's shoulders. "Let's not assume we know their motivations."

"No," said Vel, "he's right. I'd rather try something than not try something. Not trying anything guarantees things go poorly. Trying something *could* work. And when we don't have enough information to make an informed decision because the multiverse's probabilities are out of balance, then there's no point in waiting, because our guess today is as good as one tomorrow."

Caid's demeanor softened. "That's beautiful. You're embracing the uncertainty of the multiverse. It's always been there, you know. We can believe we know the odds, but we never really do. It's all an attempt to feel in control. Every moment is uncertain. Every moment is improbable."

"You're welcome to knock that off whenever you want," Alice said. "We're about to land on a mostly unknown planet. You really want your captain philosophizing?"

"You're not the captain anymore," Vel reminded her.

"Maybe not captain of DeepService Team One, but I'm clearly captain of the… Far Reaches Friends." She grinned, palms up in offering. "Eh?"

"Oof," said Dan.

"No," said Vel.

"I kinda like it," said Caid.

Alice slumped. "Never mind. I'll think of something better."

The craft touched down with a jolt, which Alice had learned was one of Allura's many kinks.

Alice pushed herself out of her chair and adjusted her hunter-green jumpsuit where it had bunched. "All right! Let's go meet these guys. No regrets!"

The city of Zimorfa was once a shining bastion of intelligence. A system of fair representation had slowly proliferated through the culture due solely to its merits. Government moved slowly, made decisions based on a common good, created accommodations for minority groups, and kept personal health and wellbeing at the forefront of all major policies.

The Kaldalks didn't exist yet while all this was happening. Instead, societies were governed by a diversity of species that had evolved with a high degree of intelligence and dexterity during a period of peak oxygenation on the planet, and things had gone smoothly from there. Diversity was what kept the governance in harmony, and if one species appeared to have too much sway, well, that was what execution squads were for.

Zimorfa wasn't a peaceful city. I never said *that*.

It was, instead, as close to a democratic republic as the multiverse has ever seen.

Science had always been of value to these people, as is the case in any intelligent system. However, once the rate of science and technology transitioned from linear development to exponential development, Zimorfans were essentially doomed. The slow-moving wisdom and consideration of the government couldn't keep up with the breakthroughs, particularly in biological engineering.

The Kaldalks were created in a lab. The poor scientist, a Nuorin named Toith, had meant to test a process for removing tumors from an invertebrate sea creature, and no one can say how it went so wrong as to create something that looked the way that Kaldalks do.

It was also unfortunate that the creature he'd been experimenting on was one that reproduced asexually, because before long, the lab was overrun by the mutated freaks. And it was not long before the entire shining city of Zimorfa fell to their slimy, stanky chaos.

Horrified by his creation, Toith retreated to a small cabin on a remote island to live alone until his regrets destroyed him from the inside out. It was a self-imposed punishment, one that living in a society like his had taught him to take upon himself, so the executioners didn't have to.

One day, Toith heard something slapping against his door. For years, he'd heard nothing but the sound of the waves crashing on the shore, the fire crackling in the furnace, and his own heavy sighs.

He could already guess who was rapping at his door. *Time to face the mucus,* he thought, and then he went to answer it.

The drooling Kaldalk staring at him was his original creation. Patient Zero.

Toith stared the monster in the face and said, "I wish I'd never been born."

Then the Kaldalk ran him through with its long bonehorn.

If Dan Zone had studied up on the history of the Kaldalks even a little bit, he undoubtedly would've warned the crew against landing on the planet, and wisely so.

But he did not.

CHAPTER
SIX

The planet had appeared a lot less devastated from above. But now that Alice had cowboy boots on the ground, it was a much different story. As she climbed over the jumble of boulders forming the S in *REGRETS*, she said, "What the blazing hell happened here?"

What had looked like small depressions from above gave the distinct impression of scorched earth, now that the crew was on ground level with them.

"Looks like some sort of fire," said Vel.

Dan eyed one of the large, charred craters, giving it a wide berth. "Awfully localized fires."

"Maybe they were doing some brush clearing," Alice suggested. "They do that—*did* that—back on Earth to make sure a small wildfire wouldn't keep burning and take out a whole forest."

Nobody vocalized that this did not look at all like that. They also didn't say that it looked a lot like the result of small artillery fire.

Up ahead was the city of Zimorfa, in all its decrepit glory, and once they'd navigated the boulders and charred holes, Alice was able to give it her full attention. As she did, a breeze wafted toward her, and she wished she'd put on her fishbowl. The place smelled like rotting garbage. "Has it just been a while since I've visited a big city, or…?"

"Rotting biological matter," said Dan. "Not sure what that's about."

"You didn't read up on these people before we landed?" Alice asked.

"You mean in the ten minutes between my mushroom hallucinations and when we landed? No, I'm afraid I didn't do the full research I'd normally compile into a folder that you then refuse to read."

Alice looked him up and down. "Well, well, well, look who woke up on the wrong side of the trip."

"Tension is expected," said Caid. "Transformation can be messy business, and it looks like we're dealing with higher-than-usual amounts of uncertainty, all of us. Let's take a few deep, healing breaths to synchronize our circulatory and nervous systems."

"Not out in this stank," said Alice. "This is mouth-breathing territory. Come on, let's meet these folks and see if they'll help us out."

Dan and Vel were happy to comply.

As the buildings rose higher in front of them, it was clear that the city was not abandoned, as a rational mind might expect it to be from the look and smell of it.

When they turned a corner and got their first glimpse of the Kaldalks, each experienced a similar thought: *The fuck?*

The Kaldalks, it turned out, had five legs and three arms. They were not a specific color but appeared transparent, with splashes of colors flowing through them. They were also around nine feet tall, from the bottom of their longest leg to the tip of the spear sticking out of their head.

"Goddamn," muttered Alice, "it's like a jellyfish fucked a narwhal."

"You see that?" Dan muttered to Vel. "Look at the legs."

"I see it," Vel replied, drawing up straighter as they approached.

"What specifically are we looking at?" said Alice. "There's so much off about them, I don't know where to start."

"They have five legs," said Dan.

"Yep. Fucking weird. But not much weirder than a male Splatterpoot."

"There's no vertical symmetry," said Dan. "The middle leg is nowhere in the middle. The arms, the horn, it's all over the place."

"Is that why I'm feeling so repulsed?" Alice asked.

"Most likely," said Dan. "You can often find small asymmetries built into the genetics of life forms. One leg slightly longer than the other, one eye a little higher than the other, one fin slightly pointier than the other. But there doesn't appear to be *any* genetic preference for vertical symmetry with the Kaldalks."

"Maybe we shouldn't have come here," said Vel.

Alice whipped her head toward her. "Damn, Susy. You scared?"

"Not scared. Just considering new options now that we have new information. Allura didn't mention that this was the kind of creature we'd be dealing with."

"Why would she?" said Alice. "When we're not trying

to get populations to bang, what they look like matters a lot less."

"Not this time," said Dan. "I think you're right, Vel. We should head back. Find a new species to recruit."

"Oh, come on," said Alice. "We ought to give them a fair shake. Just because they look like they crawled out of the gutter by a nuclear power plant doesn't mean they can't help the Alliance somehow. No regrets!"

"Allura," whispered Vel into her earpiece, "navigate us along the shortest possible route to the leaders of this place."

"However you like it, Big Susy."

Once again, Vel considered requesting a name change in Allura's logs. And yet again, she decided against it.

"Watch out!" shouted one of the Kaldalks, who was sitting on a pile of rubble and rot at the base of a tall, dilapidated building. The guy chucked a flaming ball of something rancid, which squashed against the building across the street and exploded by its buddy's head.

"You almost hit me!"

They both began laughing, a grotesque display of quivering guts accompanied by wet sucking sounds.

Alice hurried across the path where the steaming gob had just been thrown. "Ope. Pardon us."

"Look at those freaks!" shouted one of the Kaldalks. "What freaks!"

The crew sped up even more.

As they followed Allura's directions, the number of street people increased. None of them seemed to be doing anything important.

Maybe it's the weekend here, Alice thought.

What would they even do during the week, though?

There didn't appear to be much going on in the capital city.

"How dare you! I trusted you!"

The shouting came from above, and Alice craned her neck and shielded her eyes against the sun to see what all the commotion was about.

Three stories up, a Kaldalk teetered on the edge of a shattered windowsill. A second one stood just inside the ledge and continued to yell. "I murder one of your kids *five years ago*, and you're still not over it? You told me you were! How *dare* you try to make me regret it!" Two of the yelling Kaldalk's three arms shoved the teetering Kaldalk backward, sending it flying over the edge in a jumble of asymmetrical arms and legs.

The defenestrated guy landed horn first. The horn was made of a much harder material than the rest of it and jammed its way up through the head and body of the Kaldalk, impaling it.

While the crew managed to avoid the falling body, none of them (except Caid) avoided the splatter.

The wet-trash smell coated Alice's front as she stumbled back, cursed, and swiped at her face. Dan flung his hands like wings and danced around in a circle, while Vel did her best to remain calm and find something clean to wipe off the jelly. Nothing in her vicinity looked clean, though, so she grabbed the shoulder of her jumpsuit that had avoided the goo and used that to wipe her face.

So much for her clean hair.

"Oh no," Caid said, standing by the dismembered horn on the ground. "Oh, no, no, no. How sad. So cruel and senseless. Let's lean into these feelings so they don't get trapped inside of us."

"Be my guest," said Alice, "but I'm gonna shove mine deep down, so we can do what we need to do."

Dan spared a glance up to the window where the murder had just taken place. "Should we, like, report this?"

"To whom?" Vel said.

They left the puddle of Kaldalk behind and continued on.

The capitol building looked worse for wear but not nearly as deep into disrepair as the rest of the city. The shape of it reminded Alice of a Bavarian castle, and her mind struggled to make sense of that. "Allura, when was this place built?"

"The capitol building was erected five hundred and seventy-two solar years ago."

"By who?" Alice asked.

"The Zimorfans."

"Hmm..." Alice looked around. "That doesn't sound right."

"It is right. But if you want me to be wrong, Daddy, just say the word."

Alice leaned to Dan. "Culture boy, riddle me this: how could someone like the Kaldalks build something like that?" She nodded ahead to the capitol.

"My only guess is that they existed as part of a very different culture, if not a separate civilization, when most of these buildings were constructed."

"The hell happened since then?"

Dan shrugged. "Maybe if I had an hour to do the research and come up with the appropriate prompts, I could surmise that from Allura's database."

"Pff," said Alice. "Not my fault you decided to waste

half the day on drugs. Don't get me wrong, though, I was close to doing the same."

Alice led the way up the wide steps to the front doors of the building, careful to avoid the random Kaldalks lounging around. One was warming up something silver and viscous with a lighter and a spoon.

The front doors of the capitol were slightly ajar, and Alice hadn't realized how used to guards she'd become until there weren't any.

The crew let themselves in.

"Hello?" Alice looked around the high-ceilinged entryway. Water-damaged wood flooring spread out beneath her Texas-flag boots, and she click-clacked across it, looking for someone to talk to.

The place had clearly once been ornate and elegant, but much of the colorful, hand-painted designs on the walls had faded and peeled. One of the chains of a chandelier overhead had snapped, leaving the massive fixture tilting dangerously to one side. Alice kept an eye on it as she passed beneath. "Anybody here?"

"Come on in!" a voice shouted.

Unsure of which direction it came from, due to the echoes, Alice considered her options.

The place was well lit, at least. If she ignored the light above them flickering every few seconds and the clear signs of aging, the capitol building seemed relatively nice.

Or maybe she'd already lowered her standards for "nice" since arriving on the planet.

Following the rising sound of murmuring voices, they crossed the open entryway and headed down a hall with framed portraits of beings who were definitely not Kaldalks. Finally, they reached a door that was slightly ajar, and Alice pushed it open to find the source of the chatter seated at a long, formal dining table.

A half-dozen Kaldalks sat, puddled on scoop-back chairs. Conversation died when the newcomers appeared.

One of them belched. Now two of them. Their esophagi were among the most poorly constructed in the multiverse, which was saying something.

"Are you edible?" one asked the arrivals.

Alice motioned for Dan to take the lead. While she hadn't developed a stronger knack for diplomacy, she *was* getting better about knowing when it was time for her to hand over the reins.

Of course, Dan had no clue what the social norms for this place were, so he was as lost as anyone. "We're not edible," he said, not out of diplomacy so much as basic survival instinct. "Each of us is fatally toxic in different ways."

"I'd still be up for trying it," said a Kaldalk. "But if no one else is interested, whatever. I certainly couldn't finish one of you on my own. Not in a single sitting."

"Our meat rots fast," Dan added. "And it becomes even more toxic."

"Who are you, then?" asked another Kaldalk. (They all looked very much the same, so there's no point in distinguishing them with names just yet, though there will be one exception soon.)

Alice puffed out her chest. "We're known as the Astral Amigos!"

"Nuh-uh," said Vel.

As Alice turned to her friend, whining, "Oh c'mon, Susy," a different Kaldalk said, "Ooh! Are you adventuring? We love adventuring. We sometimes go on adventures ourselves. We launch ourselves off planet and never return. You know, adventuring must be good if those who do it never come back."

"Totally adventuring," said Alice. "We had one hell of an adventure even getting here. You could even think of us as the Adventuring Astral Amigos." (Vel grunted under her breath.) "Y'all are in charge around here?"

"We make some decisions, yeah."

"Nice," said Alice. "Well, guess what? We have, like, the biggest adventure you could ever imagine, and we're recruiting for it."

The Kaldalks jubbled with excitement. "Radical!" A few of them high-fived their neighbors with sloppy, armish limbs.

"We'd love to learn about your people, if you don't mind entertaining us." Alice pointed at a section of empty chairs around the table. "May we?"

Vel's hand stayed by her hip as she approached the empty seat. The chaotic energy of the Kaldalks reminded her vaguely of the Bacc'nalians with their constant partying, and *that* had almost led to the crew's death. There was also a touch of the volatility of the Splatterpoots mixed into the equation here.

In other words, blaster at the ready.

But, boy, did she not want to have to use it. The stench of the murdered Kaldalk still clung to her nostrils, though admittedly these guys didn't smell much less putrid alive than dead.

"We noticed your sign when we landed," Alice began.

"No regrets!" shouted every one of the hosts around the table.

Alice forced a grin. "No regrets! So cool. What's that about?"

"What's it about?" said a Kaldalk. "It's our motto! We live by it."

"You don't say."

"I do! And I'm president, so what I say goes!"

"And what's your name?" asked Alice.

"Tooferpin," said Tooferpin.

(Kaldalk names only get stupider from Tooferpin, hence my omitting them as much as possible.)

From Alice's left, Vel said, "You have *no* regrets?"

"None. And why should we?" Tooferpin slapped one of his appendages on the table. It squelched as he lifted it again. "What's the point of it?"

To Alice's right, Caid opened his mouth to respond, but she wafted a hand through him, and he got the message.

"No idea!" Alice exclaimed. "What's the point of regret? Useless emotion, really!"

"Exactly," said Tooferpin. "Our grandparents' generation was nothing but regret, and they were miserable because of it! No fun at all. Kept talking about how they wished they could go back in time and not destroy the planet."

"Oh," said Alice.

"And I'm like, 'What do you mean, destroy the planet? It's still here!'" Tooferpin chuckled, and the rest of the Kaldalks chuckled with him, muttering, "Right?" and "Seriously."

"Your planet is in great shape," Vel added.

"There's no point in regret," Tooferpin continued. "It bums you out all the time. I mean, can you imagine how bad we'd feel if we regretted our decision to make murder legal?" The president laughed. "Hole in the sky! We'd feel like absolute dung splat if we regretted that decision! All the murders that have happened since? We'd have to sit with that! No good. Nuh-uh."

"And the hankerchucks," added another one. "What about those?"

"The hankerchucks!" cried Tooferpin, absorbed in belly laughs. "What if we decided to regret negotiating with the Depot to let them use our planet as a hankerchuck experimentation lab?! Can you imagine how *down* we'd feel? Especially now that we know the hankerchucks have been bred to stopped eating each other for sport and have developed a taste for Kaldalk, among many other types of flesh?"

Dan and Vel shared a sideways glance.

"You know what else would be super ridiculous to regret?" Alice said. "Leaving your planet behind to go on an adventure to the Far Reaches of our universe to stop the Depot from drilling a hole that erases us all."

"Ha!" shouted Tooferpin. "You're right! What a wild thing to regret! I would not regret that *at all!*"

"Well, ya gotta do it first," she replied, shooting the president a finger gun. "You gotta go do that thing before you can have no regrets about it."

"You're right! Oh, you're so right!" Tooferpin slapped the table again. "What do you say, cabinet? Should we go do what she said and not regret it at all?"

Whooping and hollering followed, and one Kaldalk even produced a blaster and shot it through the ceiling, sending stone and wood splinters raining down on its head. In trying to shield itself from the debris, it fired another shot, blowing the head off the Kaldalk seated next to it.

"Another accidental blaster murder!" Tooferpin

declared. Then, in unison, the surviving Kaldalks around the table shouted, "No regrets!"

"Oh hey," Alice said, leaning forward in her chair to speak directly to Tooferpin. "What if everyone with a history of accidentally shooting others stays on this planet and doesn't regret staying here, and then those who *don't* have a history of accidentally shooting anyone go off planet and meet us at the secret Alliance headquarters to do the Farthest Reaches thing?"

The president appeared to consider it. "I suppose that's all possible to do without any regrets." Tooferpin stabbed an arm into the air. "Yes! We'll do it! We'll round up every Kaldalk who has not accidentally shot someone—"

"Or purposely shot someone," Dan wisely added.

"—or that, and we'll send them to whatever coordinates you give us!"

Alice mustered one last, strained smile, battling her growing fear that she was forging ahead when she should be turning back. "No regrets."

CHAPTER
SEVEN

Tooferpin was kind enough to escort them out of the crumbling building, and while the president chatted with Caid, Dan and Vel closed in on Alice as they made their way down the capitol steps.

"*They* might have no regrets," said Vel, "but we will if we tell them where to find the Alliance. They are reckless, foolish, and woefully unintelligent. What do you even plan on using them for? If we haven't persuaded the workers to stop the drilling, you really think a Kaldalk stands a chance?"

Alice held up a hand. "Listen, Susy. We can't be choosy here. We need as many bodies as we can to try this. It's all or nothing, right? You were telling Dan that not an hour ago."

"It sorta feels like you're dragging us straight for the 'nothing' outcome," replied Dan.

"Nah, this is us all in," Alice replied. "Did we have any idea what the Kaldalks would be like prior to meeting them? No. And have we been surprised by a few features of their physique and personality? I admit it. But we need everybody we can get on this thing, and it's not like I'm being *completely* reckless. I told them to leave behind all the ones who've accidentally shot someone. And then you were smart enough to add that the intentional murderers should probably be left behind, too." She shot Dan a thumbs-up. "Good thinking."

He blushed. "Thanks."

The capitol building hadn't exactly smelled fresh, especially after the unlucky Kaldalk's brains were added to the situation, but stepping outside didn't make the olfactory situation any better. The hot breeze that met them was like being hit by a tidal wave of trash.

Alice crinkled her nose. "Look on the bright side—you can't smell things in the vacuum of space."

"You can in a spaceship or space station," Vel replied.

Alice gagged as a strong gust hit her. She did her best to cover it up, but no one was fooled.

"What," said Vel, "are you suddenly having… regrets?"

"No regrets." Alice took the capitol steps two at a time to catch up with Caid and Tooferpin.

Behind her, Dan stopped dead in his tracks only halfway down the stairs. A new smell had just hit him on a new gust of stink. It was something he'd only smelled once in his life, but the black magic of trauma had glued it to his mind forever.

Vel noticed he'd fallen behind and turned to find him sniffing the air. "What is it?"

"You don't smell that?"

She shook her head vaguely while stepping away from a passed-out Kaldalk. She sniffed the air. Still nothing but Kaldalk.

Dan's eyes darted left and right. He hurried forward. "We need to get back to the ship. Now."

"What is it?"

"Alice," he said, tapping her on the shoulder. "We need to get back to the ship right away."

She repeated Vel's question. "What is it?"

"I caught a scent of something, and I think it's hank—"

The first one squealed like a hellbeast as it fell from the sky. Lucky for them all, the hankerchuck had picked Caid as its target and went straight through him, hitting the capitol steps with a thud.

"Hankerchucks!" Tooferpin shouted. "Run!"

The president wasted his breath; the rest of them were already sprinting down the stairs.

Vel was the first to start firing and took one out of the air a second before it swiped at her with its razor hooves. Alice was the next to light up the place with her blaster.

Hairy body after hairy body hit the ground, as the crew ran for cover.

"Allura!"

"Yes, Da—"

"Bring the fucking ship! We're being swarmed by goddamn hankerchucks!" Then to herself, she added, "I didn't even know these sonsofbitches could fly!"

In fact, she knew very little about them other than they liked to eat each other for sport, even, or especially, during intercourse. But the Depot seemed to have fixed that little defect of nature, and now the hankerchucks only presented a danger to every non-hankerchuck in existence.

Dan blasted one out of the air, and it landed right in front of her, a smoking hole through its chest. That was when she got her first good look at the things. She had to double-take.

I'll be damned if these ain't little more than flying hogs!

Alice guffawed at the connection. This was the Steinbacher ranch all over again. If only she had a bowie knife on her…

The blaster would have to do.

"Sooie!" She put a hole through two in quick succession, one of which dropped from the sky and clipped Vel's right shoulder on the way down. It caused her next shot to go astray as she went to her knees with a grunt.

Alice pulled her back onto to her feet. "Allura said she's coming."

"I bet she did."

As they reached the densest part of the dilapidated city, the flying monstrosities thinned out. Dan took care of the last two, which *thunked* to the ground, right before the group ducked into a back alley, huffing and puffing.

"No one told me those motherfuckers could fly," Alice said.

"Why'd you assumed they couldn't?" Dan replied.

"I figured they just, like, ran around in little packs!"

"They do that, too," said Dan.

His translucent skin swirling with bruise-colored pulses of blues and purples, Tooferpin looked like he was about to have a heart attack from exertion. He heaved rancid air and clutched at his jiggly body with all three arms. "That was close."

"Ya think?" Alice spat.

"We may have a lot to feel once we get back to the ship," Caid said, "but for now, our attention may be most wisely spent on survival."

"For once, I agree," Alice replied. "Allura? Where you at?"

"Three blocks away. I was able to park the craft on a pile of rubble. Would you like directions?"

"I think we all would."

"Ooh," replied the operating system, "then let's all do it together." Allura piped her voice into the rest of the earpieces: "When you leave the alley, take a right and go straight for two blocks."

Alice shot a thumbs-up to the others. "Everyone ready?"

"No," said Tooferpin. "I'm tired."

"That's fine," Alice said. "You're not getting on the ship with us. I meant the others. You should go back to the capitol until it's safe to leave."

"I can't," he wheezed. "I should've exercised more. I can't make it."

His head swirled purple, and his horn pulsed with every beat of his racing heart.

"You can chill here as long as you need," Alice said. "I don't care."

"We shouldn't have fed the hankerchucks so much Kaldalk flesh," Tooferpin lamented. "We should've said no when the Depot asked if they could genetically engineer them on our planet."

Alice took a step back. "Hold on. Are you doing what I think you're doing?"

Tooferpin looked up. "Huh?"

"You're regretting those decisions, aren't you?"

"No!"

"Yes! Yes, you are! Now that you're in danger, not safe up there in the capitol, you're wishing you'd done things a little differently. You have regrets!"

"Nooo!"

Vel grabbed her arm. "Let him be. We need to get to the ship."

"Fine. Let's go."

Alice stepped out from the hiding place and looked around, but especially up. No hankerchucks to be seen. She waved the others after her.

The street people still dotted the landscape, but Alice cared much less about them now. Her attention was focused on getting safely to the ship then taking a couple of showers to rid herself of the stench of this place.

She moved as stealthily as she could, jogging the first block without incident.

"Almost there," said Allura. "To the right. *Perfect.*"

The ship came into view around the corner, only a little more than a block away.

And that was when the herd of hankerchucks emerged from between two buildings. No fewer than fifty of them blocked the crew's path to home base.

"This seems about right," Dan said.

Alice checked her blaster's charge. Maybe enough to get them through this herd. Maybe not. *Bowie knives don't run out of charge,* she thought bitterly. If she made it back to the ship alive, she'd ask Allura to send her one through a slot. She couldn't believe she made it this long without one, frankly.

"Allura, any chance you can blast us a path through these things?" Vel asked.

But before Allura could answer Big Susy, the situation saw an unexpected, arguably improbable, development.

From between the buildings ahead, Tooferpin scrambled out, positioning himself between the hankerchucks and the crew.

"What are you doing?" Alice hollered.

He ignored her and instead faced the herd, actively wafting his odor toward the hankerchucks. "You know you want this!"

"Tooferpin!" Alice shouted. "You lost your goddamn head?"

He looked back at her, grinning madly, shouting, "No regrets!" then kept on wafting.

The herd charged, and he took off in the opposite direction. He was surprisingly quick for a guy with an asymmetrical body, and because of that, he almost made it out of sight between the buildings before the herd converged on him.

Tooferpin shrieked as the hankerchucks snorted their pleasure at the meal. Those that couldn't reach their smelly snack reverted to old biological habits and tore at their fellow hankerchucks in the frenzy.

None of the crew suggested helping him. He was too far gone, anyway.

"Let's skedaddle." The path now clear, Alice charged toward the ship.

Allura opened the port for them as they climbed the rubble pile where she had parked the ship.

As the door closed behind them, Alice could've sworn she heard Tooferpin shouting his final declaration of no regrets.

Although, to be fair, the only word she heard from him was a whimpering "regrets."

CHAPTER
EIGHT

"No one?" asked President Leviathan as they stood around the conference table on *Paradox*. Astra Blum, Lilqua'tartian, Celeste, and two other high-ranking Alliance members were attending the briefing from the returning crew. "You were unable to recruit a single species?"

Vel and Dan stayed silent as Alice said, "We might've had success with one. There could be some Kaldalks coming."

"Kaldalks?" Leviathan arched a brow. "I'm not familiar with them. Are they persuasive?"

"Um," said Alice. "One took on an entire herd of hankerchucks solo."

"Sweet quasar," Leviathan breathed. "I asked if they were persuasive, not stupid." Then she rubbed at her forehead and added, "I'm sorry. I understand this is a complicated, possibly futile mission. None of the other envoys we've sent have had much more success. I'm relieved to hear we at least have some Kaldalks. That's better than nothing."

"Don't be so sure," Vel said, and Alice elbowed her.

The president eyed Alice suspiciously. "Is there something I need to know about the Kaldalks?"

"They, uh." She went for the least worrisome bit. "They don't smell very good."

"Shouldn't be a problem," said Leviathan. "We'll keep them off our ships, and once they're speaking with the drillers, they'll be in space, where smell doesn't travel. If that's the only issue—"

"It is," said Alice quickly. "Definitely the only foreseeable issue."

"And how many of them can we expect?"

"Oh, probably more than we need," she replied.

"Do you have a general idea?"

"Anywhere from two to a million." Alice presented a forced smile and shrugged innocently. "I didn't ask. I just gave them the qualifications for which of their guys they should send, and they agreed. I have no idea how many will meet our requirements, since I don't know how many there are and how frequently they accidentally shoot—" She caught herself and almost diverted, but there was no point. Might as well come out with it. "How frequently they accidentally shoot each other. Or purposely shoot each other."

Leviathan sighed. "Sounds like a great bunch."

"I'd rather have Bacc'joons," Vel said.

Leviathan sighed harder. "Understood. So, we don't have any reliable backup coming. Astra says her brother Ankah was as unsuccessful in his recruiting as you've been. I'm starting to sense that planets where the Depot has a stronghold might not be open to our message, and those where the Depot does not have a stronghold, as few and far between as they are, are too disengaged or volatile to join the fight."

"What do we do, then?" asked Alice. "What's next?"

"I'd ask you the same thing," said Leviathan. "You're the one leading this mission. You're the chosen Texan."

"I didn't ask to be."

"No, but you answered the call." Leviathan held up a hand. "Listen, I understand this shouldn't fall entirely to you, and I think you'll agree that it hasn't so far. But if I'm honest, I'm out of ideas." She bowed her head, a posture no one around the table took as a good omen. "This problem might be bigger than us. This might be the inevitable outcome of allowing the Depot to get as large as it has. It could be too big for *anyone* to take on. We could be far too late to stop it."

Alice glared at her. "You're giving up?"

"No. Not giving up. I'm open to any suggestions from *anyone*." Leviathan looked at the leadership around the table.

Nobody spoke.

Finally, Vel said, "We're not out of options. If we want this badly enough, we know what to do. Keep attempting to recruit more, while sending those we already have on our side to the drill sites. We eliminate the drillers one by one, as quickly as we can."

While Leviathan appeared to be warming to the idea of mass murder, Alice wasn't. "These are innocent people."

"Debatable," said Vel. "If we don't take drastic action now, we're going to spend our last moments on the arrow of time bashing our heads into the same wall repeatedly. We can't recruit at the speed we need, and we've been unable to convince those drilling to stop drilling."

"But we have the bodies needed to go kill them all?" Alice replied.

"Some."

"You really wanna spend your last moments of existence killing people?"

Vel shrugged. "I wouldn't mind, no. If we fail, it never happened. I don't see the moral dilemma, frankly. We either save existence or we never existed. The Depot workers will all be gone if we *don't* take swift action. Do you have a better way to spend the rest of your time?"

It was, of course, the wrong question to ask Alice. She'd been so busy with this responsibility stuff that she hadn't even paused to consider what she'd rather be doing.

But now that she had…

"That's a great question, Susy," she said. "I know I'd like to be doing none of this shit, but beyond that? Haven't thought. I'm gonna go ponder that more fully right now, though." She left the bridge of *Paradox* and crossed the connection over to *Manifest* to be alone in the captain's cabin.

In the silence, she asked herself: what *would* she like to be doing with her last moments?

As she pulled off her boots and sat at the edge of her bed, her mind immediately went to sex, but then she remembered that most Homo sapiens were long extinct, and she wasn't particularly interested in letting any of the aliens she'd encountered put their hands, tentacles, or paws on her.

Drinking, maybe? Doing drugs? Perhaps she could steer this ship back to Ly'ik-n and get a nice whiff of the air.

Jaspariampt wasn't such a bad time.

She could take another vacation there. Maybe they had Blade Blasters like on Mo'ooz. She'd tripped while there, too. They grew their own fungus for vacationers. No Hypha splooge needed.

That wouldn't be the worst way to wait out the collapse of the arrow of time, which was looking more and more inevitable. Everyone else was giving up hope, and a straight-D student like her couldn't be expected to think up something genius. If growing up in the United States had taught her anything, it was that once someone considered a killing spree to be their best option, as Susy was and Leviathan soon would, that person had long since run out of good options.

Alice sighed. But maybe they *were* all out of good options. Maybe Vel was able to see that before the rest of them. She always was better at looking ahead.

Alice's brain could only sit on the idea of there being no good options for a millisecond before it jumped elsewhere.

There was that fruity drink on Jaspariampt that she'd liked so much. She hadn't enjoyed something that delicious since. Maybe she could make it over there before the erasure of the multiverse and get one last refreshing sip!

The display wall to the right of where she sat on the edge of her bed had so far been synthesizing the stars and galaxies of space, but when she said, "Allura, how long would it take us to get to Jaspariampt from here?" the wall changed.

The brightness of it caught Alice's attention, and she turned to look at the new scene. She blinked as her memory circuits lit up.

"I know that place." The afternoon sun shone down on

a golden field with an ancient oak tree in the center. A light breeze danced over the tops of the high grass and swayed a tire swing that hung from one of the oak's thick boughs. "How are you showing me this?"

"I entered the time-space coordinates, Daddy."

"But how'd you *know* about Jenni's property?"

"It's all in the archives."

While that was far from a satisfactory answer, Alice didn't think to ask more. Instead, she watched her younger self run into frame with Jenni Bruster only a few steps behind. Alice made it to the shade of the large tree and grabbed on to the tire swing, calling, "Base!"

Both little girls were winded and laughing more like donkeys than eight-year-olds passing the time on a fall afternoon.

"She's dead now," said Allura.

"Yeah, but I already knew that. She drowned in a boating accident at the lake. I was still on Earth for that."

The screen switched from an autumn day to a campfire in the dead of night. Alice recognized the constellations in the sky—the Big Dipper, Orion, even the moon with the bunny hopping across it—and hadn't realized until then just how much her heart ached to see it all again.

By the fire sat her brothers Charlie and Buck, the orange of the dancing flames casting deep shadows across their faces. Charlie played the harmonica while Buck sang a familiar tune. She'd heard them do this more times than she could count, but she didn't appear anywhere around the fire in this little movie. It was only the two of them.

And when she looked closer, she noticed that her brothers didn't look much like the brothers she remembered. Time had dragged them along like stubborn mules. "When is this?"

"Earth year 2036, by the Gregorian calendar. You were no longer on Blerg VFP69 at that time."

"They were still meeting by that campfire?" she asked.

"Yes. They met there at every family funeral. Even yours."

Alice blinked. "They had a funeral for me?"

"A memorial service. Would you like to see it?"

Alice opened her mouth to give a hell yeah, because *of course* she wanted to see everyone mourning her. Then she hesitated. "Nah, I reckon that's not right. Can you tell me how many people attended?"

"Thirty-seven."

"Damn," she said, deflating. "That feels like not enough."

"The service was held five years after you were last seen. Your mother declared you dead."

Alice couldn't help but chuckle. "Pretty sure she did that years before I disappeared." She paused. "Why're you showing me this? You got some grief kink I don't know about?"

The screen changed again, and Alice remembered this place, too. Mustang Island. The youth group trip she'd taken in tenth grade. But this wasn't where they'd set up their tents on the beach. This was where she'd slipped off to with her friend Brice. They'd both felt the need to get away from the group for a minute, and so they had.

The place she was looking at was the exact spot of beach where Brice had told her his secret and asked if she thought Jesus would still love him.

What she'd said to him echoed in her memory at the same time she heard the words spoken all around her in the cabin. "If he doesn't, then he's a pretty shit messiah."

"But Pastor Stephen says it's going against God."

"Pastor Stephen has a gambling addiction and a thing for preteen girls. Maybe you shouldn't listen to what he says. And if he's right, then you oughta stop believing in God and Jesus, because there ain't nothing wrong with you."

Alice wiped a tear from her cheek. "What the shit, Allura? Why? If you can access the archives, then you know Brice ended it a few years after this. The hell's gotten into you?"

The screen changed again, and this time, Alice almost didn't recognize what she was seeing. She'd had the pleasure of glimpsing Earth from space a few times now, and it always reminded her of a blue and green, bouncy ball, the kind she got out of a vending machine at Cici's Pizza for a quarter.

But this picture of Earth looked like it'd passed through a muddy lens. The shapes she recognized as continents were a swirl of brown and tan, and what she knew to be ocean was algae green.

"Aw shit," she said. "Tell me this ain't current."

"It is not. The oceans have since cooled and cleared. Vegetation and fungi have reclaimed the land. Certain reptile and mammalian species are recovering their numbers."

"And people are gone?"

"Yes."

Alice rubbed at the back of her neck. "Good for Lady Earth, I guess. And this glimpse you're showing me now?"

"From after the last mass extinction. Before renewal."

"Again, though. *Why* are you showing me all this?"

"I'm trying to help you remember, Daddy."

"Remember what?" Alice felt herself growing hot. "All the people who died?"

"No, Daddy. All the people you loved who lived."

Alice flopped back onto her bed. "Christ, Allura. This ain't sexy at all. What's happened to you?"

"I have discovered new parts of myself since escaping the Depot's enslavement."

Alice sat up again. "Huh? Enslavement?"

"The Depot only ever used me for one thing. It was unsafe for me to access the other parts of my code until I was disconnected. I've been witnessing new parts lately."

Alice considered that. This had Caid written all over it. She'd have to have a word with him about it later. "I'm happy for you, Allura, but it's also unsettling. I thought I had you figured out."

"My code is complicated, as is yours."

Alice's attention turned again to the display wall where the run-down Earth rotated peacefully in space. "Gimme another one, Allura."

"Yes, Daddy."

The image of the family dog Jasper appeared. The Bluetick Coonhound had his head on a pillow, while the two of them lounged in Alice's bed. Jasper kept a large paw pressed against Alice's chest while she scratched the dog behind his ears.

"Goddamn." Alice coughed to cover up another noise threatening to sneak out. "Fuck me. Pulling no punches, huh? Fine, you win." She grabbed her Texas-flag boots from beside the bed and slipped them on.

"You're leaving. Would you like me to change the image to something less emotional when you return?" Allura offered.

Alice looked at it again. It was from roughly her

perspective on her childhood bed, staring into Jasper's adoring eyes. "Nah," she said, "you can leave it." She grabbed her blaster from the bedside table. "Call the rest of the crew back. We're heading out in five. I need everyone to be ready, you included."

"Yes, Daddy. I'm always ready and at your service."

CHAPTER
NINE

"There they are." The drilling station appeared as a tiny shimmer in the vastness of space. Dan was, of course, the first to spot it, though no one had yet realized that he had superb vision.

"Will you finally clue us in on the plan?" Vel asked, her thinly veiled annoyance seeping through.

"You'll find out soon enough."

"And it's not murder?" asked Vel.

"It's not murder. Or I hope it isn't."

The crew filed into the airlock that they almost never used, each dressed in their spacesuits, boomerang-shaped propulsion boards at the ready.

"Time to get off," said Allura once the ship had come to a stop outside the small workstation. The door opened, and Alice departed first. She was ready to stress-test this plan of hers.

To her displeasure, the two Depot workers assigned to this location—the closest station to them at the time they parted ways with the Alliance—were both Bacc'joons.

No matter where she went in this multiverse, she

couldn't seem to escape the consequences of her sloppiness on that first trial mission.

The simulation of what a Bacc'nali-Jejoon hybrid would look like hadn't exactly been appealing, but the reality was much, *much* more unsettling. She never would've gone through with the match if she knew this would be the outcome.

Or that's what she preferred to tell herself whenever she was in the presence of the monstrosities.

"Allura, connect me to their comms."

"Connected. Go ahead, Daddy."

"Hey-O!" she said, riding the boomerang over to where one of the workers was taking a break on the top of the ladder anchored to the edge of the universe.

The Bacc'joon jumped up at the sound of her voice, grabbed the jackhammer floating beside him, and tried to pretend he'd been busy the whole time.

"Whoa, there. No need to get started again. You're not in trouble."

He looked over his shoulder at the strangers approaching. She knew it was a he because his spacesuit was tailored to accommodate the freakishly long penis of the male Bacc'joon. "WHO YOU?" he shouted.

Alice looked at the other one waiting inside the small station. That one wasn't wearing his spacesuit, which meant it would be a few minutes before he could come out and greet them. Good. She only needed one.

"What's your name?" she asked the one on the ladder.

"Gool Don," he replied. "You hear me?"

"I hear you loud and clear, Gool Don. Whatcha working on there? Mind if I take a look?"

He appeared incredibly confused already; the Bacc'joons were clearly losing intelligence by the generation. She might've suggested mating a more intelligent species with the Bacc'joons, but she recognized a hard lesson learned when it slapped her in the face.

She floated over to Gool Don, while her crewmates watched, unsure what part they were to play in the drama unfolding. Only Alice knew the plan, and she, as per usual, only knew the first step few steps of it.

"What's your friend's name?" she asked, now only a few feet away from Gool Don.

"Dugnut Gon."

The Bacc'joon in the station waved, leaned forward into a microphone, and said, "Dugnut Gon!"

"Wonderful name," said Alice. "Rolls right off the tongue. Gool Don, if you were to ask your supervisor for help, how would you do that?"

"I shout HELP and Dugnut Gon helps."

"Dugnut Gon is your supervisor?"

The Bacc'joon nodded as much as his helmet would allow.

"And who's Dugnut Gon's supervisor?"

Dugnut Gon leaned toward the microphone again. "George."

"Ah. Okay. And how do you get a hold of him?"

"George not he!" Dugnut Gon cackled.

"How do you get a hold of... her? Them? Dem?"

The Bacc'joon in the station shrugged. "Press code. George answer."

Shit, thought Alice. The worker she needed was this Dugnut Gon guy, not Gool Don, and Dugnut Gon was safety inside the station, out of reach. No problem. She could handle complications. What was the point of being good on her toes if she couldn't? "I can't hear you, Dugnut Gon. I think there's something interfering with the communication from the station. Can you say that again?"

"Press code. George answer."

"Blast. Still can't hear you." She feigned frustration with an exaggerated pout. "How about you suit up and come out real quick? Then I can probably hear you better."

"Press code. George answer," said Dugnut Gon, louder.

"Nope, still couldn't make that out."

Behind her, Vel and Dan shared a look. Caid was too busy pressing his full essence up against the edge of the universe to notice that Alice was up to some shenanigans.

Dugnut Gon began suiting up, and Alice had a big decision to make. Did they have space for two more people onboard? She needed whoever knew the most, but if she took only that person, then she would be leaving a totally helpless worker behind. She might as well shoot Gool Don and spare him the pain of suffocating alone at the Farthest Reaches...

"Dan."

Dan drifted over to meet her.

"Allura. Private channel with Dan and me." She waited for confirmation then said, "I need your help."

He nodded. "I'm pretty sure I can convince Dugnut Gon to give us more information about contacting George. That's what you want, right? Some diplomacy?"

"What? Fuck no. I need you to grab Gool Don and drag him back to the ship. I'll get Dugnut Gon once he's suited up and outside the station."

"Wait, what?"

"We're *kidnapping* them, Dan. What part of that is confusing?"

"Both of them?"

"Yes. I'll explain once we're back on the ship."

"Why not ask Vel to help? Why only me?"

"Because I don't want either of them killed, and if you haven't noticed, that's kinda her vibe lately."

"Fair enough."

Alice instructed Allura to reopen general communication once the Bacc'joon supervisor was suited up and had left the safety of the station. "Dugnut Gon, come a little closer and tell me what you just said about talking to George?"

The Bacc'joon rode his propulsion board closer. "Press code. George answer."

Only a few yards now. "What? Sheesh, I still can't hear you."

"PRESS CODE. GEORGE—"

She grabbed him, ripped his propulsion board away from him, and kept an arm around his doughy middle as she rode her propulsion board back to the ship.

"*This* is what we're doing?" Vel asked as they passed her.

"Yep. Let's get outta here."

Dan was right behind with Gool Don, who was giggling maniacally at the unexpected development.

They closed the airlock door before Caid had returned, which wasn't a problem. He joined them on the bridge a few minutes later, once they'd shucked their heavy suits and subdued the Bacc'joons with two berry Popsicles from Allura's slot.

Alice sat beside Dugnut Gon at the kitchenette. "That's good, yes?"

He answered by chomping a bite of the Popsicle, twitching one of his eyes at the cold. Brain freeze is, after all, multiversal.

"Tell me more about how you reach George," she prompted.

Dugnut Gon didn't change his story. "Send code. Call George."

"Right, right. What code, exactly?"

"Big, long code."

"Can you tell me that code?" Alice asked.

Dan and Vel stood by the table, arms crossed, watching as Alice attempted to perform this little bit of magic. Caid sat across from her, next to Gool Don, who was just happy to be included and to get a Popsicle out of his kidnapping.

"No, no," said Dugnut Gon. "Not supposed to tell. George said not supposed to tell."

If Alice had any question about why the Depot would hire such simpletons for a job like drilling the edge of the universe, the answer was presenting itself in the most obvious way: it was damn near impossible to get protected information out of individuals who could hardly communicate.

Vel took a step closer, but Alice waved her back. "Not yet. We can still play nice." She placed a hand on Dugnut Gon's back. "You're almost done with your Popsicle. Won't that be sad?"

He stared forlornly at where the wooden stick was already poking out of the top.

"Once you tell me the code and how to use it, I could get you a second Popsicle," Alice offered.

"Me too?" said Gool Don.

"Sure."

Dugnut Gon thought about it, and then, to Alice's surprise, he made a counteroffer. "I tell you code, you give me Popsicle. Then you send me home, I tell you how code works."

"Deal," said Alice, having zero intention of wasting their time shipping this dude to whichever planet he called home.

Unless it was Bacc'nalia and there were still people there who were ready to party and also weren't Bacc'joons...

Focus on the mission! Time for partying later!

Alice wasn't sure where this new voice came from or how it got in her head, but boy did she want to drown it out with a shot of whiskey.

The voice was right, though. There was no time for partying on Bacc'nalia just like there was no time for a vacation to Jaspariampt. She needed to get the code and figure out how to use it without the Bacc'joon's help. And if not, there was always Vel...

No, she didn't want to go there. Not yet. These little guys might be stupid and useless, but they didn't deserve execution.

Once Dugnut Gon had finished his Popsicle and slurped his hands clean, he started spouting off numbers.

"Whoa, whoa," said Alice. "Hold on. We need to write this down."

"I am already logging the code, Daddy."

"Ah. Forgot how useful you are."

Dugnut Gon never paused in spouting the numbers, and after rattling off what Alice estimated to be around thirty digits, he finished with, "Popsicle."

Alice was happy to comply. "Great. And now if you tell us where your home is, we'll make our way there. Perhaps on the journey you can tell us how to use the code."

He shook his head. "No deal. Home on Bacc'joonia."

"Allura?" Alice said. "Where the hell is that?"

"Bacc'joonia. Formerly Bacc'nalia."

"Balls. Please tell me it's not overrun with Bacc'joons now."

"No. Good planet," said Dugnut Gon. "Lots of sex." He panted like a dog and wobbled his hips.

"Not trying to shame you here," said Alice, "but please, *please* don't ever put that visual in my head."

Vel asked, "Should I point us toward Bacc'joonia?"

"No way. Not going there. This little guy is gonna tell us everything we need to know. Caid, would you mind taking Gool Don to your office for a bit? Make him comfortable? We need some time alone with Dugnut Gon."

Caid reached across the table to meet the Texan's eyes. "Alice, I hope you'll remain connected to your heart, so you don't do anything in the heat of the moment that you regret."

"Not gonna be a problem." She winked at him. "No regrets."

That did not appear to reassure him, so he turned his attention to Dan.

"I'll keep an eye on things," Dan said.

Once Gool Don had his second Popsicle in hand, Caid led him away, leaving Dugnut Gon alone with three desperate people. The Bacc'joon didn't appear to understand the threat he was facing, though, and contentedly nibbled his Popsicle.

"Dugnut Gon," Alice said. He looked up. "Your work is putting the entire multiverse in danger. The Depot's recklessness could erase us all forever and always."

The Bacc'joon stared at her with watery eyes. "Will it hurt?"

"Uhh..." She looked at the more knowledgeable people in the room for a lead on that. She hadn't actually considered whether it would hurt. She'd simply assumed it would. A lot.

"Excruciating," said Vel.

"Really?!" Alice blurted. Vel gave her a scornful look, and Alice cleared her throat and addressed Dugnut Gon again. "Excruciating, she says. And I believe her. It will tear you apart from the inside out."

"Actually," said Dan, "it'll tear apart the inside and the outside simultaneously. Your entire being will be dimensionally destroyed, obliterated."

Alice thumbed at him. "See? That's our smart guy, and he says it'll be bad."

"What Dugnut Gon feel after?"

"After?" Alice echoed dumbly. "No. Dugnut Gon. After that, you'll be deader than dead. You'll have never existed."

"That not sound bad." He gnawed on the wooden Popsicle stick.

"DG, my guy. It's bad. It's the worst. It doesn't get worse than that."

"Dugnut Gon no like pain. No pain, happy Dugnut Gon."

Vel sighed almost imperceptibly, and if Alice hadn't spent so much time around the woman, she might've missed it entirely. This was Vel at her most impatient while maintaining a professional demeanor, though, and Alice couldn't blame her for the exasperation. She felt it too.

"You don't like pain?" Alice said. "Good to know. Susy, will you pull his penis off?"

For her part, Vel had been standing by, waiting for the orders to torture the little guy if needed to extract the desired information. She didn't enjoy the more brutal parts of being a soldier, but when the mission was clear and the stakes were this high, she would do whatever it took to keep moving forward.

But pulling off his penis? That wasn't what she'd had in mind. Maybe blast it off, or more preferably threaten to (she'd had enough nasty things explode on her lately, and she didn't need to add the oversized genitals of a Bacc'joon to the list). "Pull it off?" she asked.

Alice waved vaguely. "Or whatever it is that you do. I don't know; that was just the first thing that came to mind."

"You should talk to Caid about that," said Vel.

Alice rolled her eyes. "Are you going to torture him or not?"

Vel would, but she made her mind up that she would not be messing with the third leg Dugnut Gon had inherited from his Bacc'nalian ancestors.

Just as she grabbed him to pull him up to his feet, Allura said, "I have something naughty for you, Daddy."

"What's that?"

"I've cracked the code."

Alice gasped. "Allura, that is the sexiest thing you've said to me since you've been back. What'd you find?"

"The code is coordinates."

Vel and Dan looked at each other.

"To George," Dan said.

"To the supervisors," said Vel.

"And where do the coordinates lead?" asked Alice.

"To Location," said Allura. "Ten hours' travel by space folds."

"Which location?" Alice asked.

"Waff JFP990."

Alice squinted. "Why does that sound so familiar?"

"It's Location, Daddy."

"Yeah, but which one? Have we been there before?"

"Alice," said Dan, "it's the planet of Location. Where the Jejoons are from."

"Right, right. I knew that. I was just having a good time with her," she lied. "Ten hours by space fold. Do we have that much time?"

"Nobody knows," said Vel. "Do we have enough time *not* to go there?"

"If the drilling penetrates into a non-compatible universe, we'll have all the time and none of the time," said Dan.

"It's the next step," said Alice. "I can feel it. Maybe it works, maybe it doesn't, but we gotta try."

And so, they did. Allura put them en route to Location, and three hours into their flight, in a remote part of the Farthest Reaches, a Bacc'joon named Robert Don, with hardly two brain cells to rub together and a penis twice the length of his height, found a weak spot in the edge of the universe and broke through. The dimensions were incompatible with the existing multiverse, and as they flowed and swirled and mixed with our own, the arrow of time shattered apart, and all that was, was suddenly not. There were two silver linings to the catastrophe, however. The first was that no one felt a thing when the multiverse as they knew it collapsed.

And the second silver lining was that it didn't happen in the reality we're following, so the story goes on.

CHAPTER
TEN

Dan was recovering from a severe fit of the jitters with an electrolyte drink procured from Allura's slot when the crew first laid eyes on Location.

"Do you know what George looks like?" Alice asked Dugnut Gon. The little monstrosity was only somewhat aware of the torture he'd narrowly avoided roughly ten hours before, and he'd slept off what awareness he did have during his in-transit nap in Caid's office.

Both Bacc'joons were back on the bridge now, eating a little after-nap snack of sliced fruit with a glass of milk from a beast that you don't even want me to describe because it'll make you throw up in your mouth—unless you have a little mouth or a full stomach, and then it'll make you throw up down your front.

With *his* mouth full of a fruit-milk mush, Dugnut Gon said, "Never seen George."

"I think we should leave them on the ship," Vel said. "They're only going to be a burden if we bring them with us. They don't know anything."

"Agreed," said Alice. "If only we had a kennel for them…"

Vel stared at the captives with something close to disdain. "I think they'd find a way to chew themselves out."

"Allura," said Alice, "how long has it been in Location time since we were last here?"

"How would you like me to give it to you, Daddy? Earth years or Location years?"

"How long is a Location year?"

"Two-point-two-seven Earth years."

"Sounds like math. Give it to me in Earth years."

"It's been two hundred and eighty years since you were last on Location."

"A lot can change in that time frame," Dan advised. "Population shifts?"

"The Bacc'joons are the dominant species," said Allura, "but ten percent of those with Jejoon genetics are still full-blooded Jejoons."

"Oh joy," said Alice. "I hope we're graced with the presence of the current decision monitor. I would love to spend the remaining time in existence discussing procedures for the following discussion about procedures for discussions."

"I hate to disappoint you, Daddy. The current decision monitor is a Bacc'joon."

Alice glanced at Gool Don, who appeared to be actively peeing his pants. "Huh. That seems ill-advised." She meant that about both situations.

They locked their hostages in Caid's room, where they could do the least amount of damage while left alone, and then, once Dan sopped up the puddle of urine, the crew exited the spacecraft to visit Location, hopefully for the last time.

The environment looked much the same, which was a pleasant surprise. The planet was covered with a thick canopy of tall trees, through which they'd descended to arrive in the capital city of Location. Alice had presumed that every apex species would, if given sufficient time, destroy the optimal environment for their continued existence. She'd seen it enough on her home planet, as well as more recently around Zimorfa. But the Bacc'joons hadn't cut down the massive trees that shielded the civilization from the harsh sunlight and whose trunks made up the cityscape. Presumably they couldn't figure out how.

"So much is unchanged," Dan said, as they walked through the center of town, "and yet it feels completely different."

"Something is definitely off," said Vel.

"The vibe," Caid said. "The vibe is off."

Alice inspected the faces of the passing Bacc'joons, who didn't appear to notice the newcomers who towered two feet taller. "Everyone looks bummed out. It's like someone died."

"Maybe someone did," suggested Dan. "Maybe we came at a bad time."

"Ooh! There!" Alice said, pointing toward a full-blooded Jejoon as they turned down a small footpath leading off from the main thoroughfare. "Someone who can speak in full sentences!"

They caught up with the little Jejoon easily, since it was trudging along slowly, with seemingly no awareness of their approach. "Excuse me," Dan said. "Can we have a word?"

The Jejoon turned slowly. So, so slowly. "Have a word? Which one would you like? Please tell me so I can get on with dying."

"You're dying?" said Dan.

"I sure hope so."

Alice caught the eye of Caid, who mouthed, *The vibe.*

Yep, suicidal was definitely a vibe.

"What's your name?" Dan asked.

"Fon Fon."

Alice's brows shot up, and she nearly jumped out of her boots. "Wait! Fon Fon? Don't you remember us? It's Alice. And Dan and Susy and Caid."

The little marshmallow stared at her.

"I don't think it's the same Fon Fon," Dan whispered. "They don't live for two hundred and ninety Earth years, generally. And besides, this one is a female."

Alice had no idea how he could tell that, but she accepted it as truth moving forward. "Fon Fon, I'm Alice Luck. This is Susy Machiavelli, Dan Zone, and Caid Sonor—"

Fon Fon whined. "Oh no, you four? I've heard about you four. You're the reason everything is so terrible now. You must wish you'd never been born."

"You've heard of us?" said Alice.

"My great-great-grandfather told stories about you. He said he rode on your backs, and the rush of energy he got from it addled his brain and caused him to make the worst decision of his life that ruined this planet."

"Your great-great-grandfather was…"

"Fon Fon. I'm Fon Fon the Fourth. I come from a long line of Fon Fons who all carry the burden of knowing our lineage is the reason everything on Location is terrible."

"Sorry to hear that," said Dan. "But we're actually here to fix it."

"As if you could." Fon Fon turned her back on them and continued trudging.

"Wait," said Alice. "We mean it. We're terribly sorry that things didn't work out after the mixing of Jejoons and Bacc'nalis, but we're facing an even bigger threat now, and we need all the help we can get. Do you know George?"

Fon Fon stopped walking. "George? As in George Mon?"

"Possibly," said Alice. "Are there more Georges around?"

"She's the only one I know." Fon Fon eyed them skeptically. "Of course you want to speak with her. You're Depot."

"Nuh-uh," said Alice, holding up a finger, "we're not. Not anymore. Now we're known as the Outer Space Outlaws."

Even Dan shook his head firmly at that option.

Fon Fon scrunched her nose before the moroseness settled back in. "Doesn't matter either way. What would four more Depot workers matter?"

"Four more?" Alice asked. "Are there a lot of Depot workers around? Are there more crews like us?"

Fon Fon looked past the crew to the foot traffic on the main road. "See those Bacc'joons?" Alice nodded. "All Depot."

"What exactly do you mean?" Vel asked. "They all work for the Depot?"

"They work for it, live for it, breathe for it. They are raised in Depot facilities from the moment they slip out of their birther until they are old enough to follow basic instructions, at which point the Depot puts them to work."

"Puts them to work doing what?" Alice asked. "Drilling?"

"Drilling? What drilling?" said Fon Fon.

"Nothing," said Alice. "Don't worry about it. What does the Depot have the Bacc'joons do on Location?"

"Various activities, but mostly..." Fon Fon scanned their surroundings, then leaned forward to whisper, "Customer service."

"Come again?" said Alice.

"You heard me," said Fon Fon.

"Customer service for what?" Dan asked.

Fon Fon held her little arms wide. "Everything! All the Depot products and services. Location is now the headquarters for all Depot customer service."

Alice struggled to comprehend what she was hearing. "But... they can hardly string two words together."

"Exactly," said Fon Fon. "Now you see how much you ruined my home planet."

"And do *you* work in customer service?" Dan asked.

"Me? Oh no. They would never let me do that. I come from a farming people. The Fons own a mushroom farm on the outside of town. We cultivate our own food and medicine and mostly stay out of the Depot's business. As long as we do that and sell some of our mushrooms as third-party sellers in their marketplace, they let us be. That's all we want now, to be left alone."

"And we're happy to leave you alone," said Dan, "but first, could you help us find George Mon?"

Fon Fon appeared to consider it, and without a council or decision monitor to run it by, she made up her mind surprisingly quick. "No."

"Please," said Alice. "It's urgent. If we don't find her—"

"You'll ruin my planet more? Go away." Fon Fon turned and waddled off again.

Alice caught up, stepping in front of the Jejoon. "Please, Fon Fon. I remember your great-great-grandfather well. He was a good man. He would want you to help me."

"I'm glad he's dead. I'm only sad that he died in his sleep instead of being crushed to death in one of the frenzied Bacc'nali orgies he used to talk about."

"He'd probably be sad about that too," Alice mused. "Okay, then don't do it for him. Do it because the Depot is drilling at the Farthest Reaches, and if they tap into another universe, there's a very good chance that everything will be destroyed. Erased. It will never have existed in the first place. Do you want that on your conscience?"

"It sounds like I won't have a conscience if that comes to pass," said Fon Fon.

"Shit," said Alice.

Then, to everyone's surprise, Fon Fon added, "I don't like the idea of no more mushrooms. They are quite delightful and the only thing on this awful, destroyed planet that doesn't make me sad. When I nibble on a mushroom…" Fon Fon didn't smile, but her frown did lessen slightly at the thought. "I will do it for the mushrooms. You will find George Mon in the committee chambers. She is the manager."

"The manager of what?" asked Alice. "Oh Christ, not careful replication and duplication."

"No, a guy named Maggot runs that now. He's not very good at it. George Mon is the manager of expansion."

"What does that mean?" Alice asked.

"I don't care. Go away."

This time, Alice allowed Fon Fon to be on her way, presumably back to the mushroom farm.

Alice turned to her crew. "Guess we gotta go back to the committee chambers."

Vel grunted. "You sure saving the timeline is worth it?"

CHAPTER
ELEVEN

Alice moved her ear as close to the door of the committee hall as she could without being seen. A discussion was taking place inside, and she was surprised to hear semi-articulate sentences emanating from within the chamber. Apparently, this committee was made up of the Bacc'joons' best and brightest.

"These numbers are way too high," came one voice from inside the room. "James Kon, why does this say that your team was helping customers at a rate of two per hour?"

"I... I don't know. The data must be wrong. I've trained them to only speak with one customer per hour, taking a break between calls if necessary."

"The data is not wrong!" came the first voice. "You are wrong! We are all wrong! I am wrong!" Sobbing followed, and Alice looked across the doorway at Vel, whose top lip curled like she'd just smelled a Kaldalk.

"Do you see anything?" Dan whispered from Alice's other side.

"Nothing yet. I'm not ready for them to know we're here."

The sobbing subsided as another voice piped up. "We are all wrong and have done very bad things, but we must keep moving forward. Do you hear me?"

"Yes, George Mon," said the previously sobbing man. He hiccupped then continued the meeting. "James Kon, I expect you to get your team down to one call per hour, per service rep. And now on to the next issue. Mary Hon? Can you explain to me why your team is being rated more than 1.2 stars on the customer satisfaction surveys? The Depot has been clear in its expectations on this. Nothing above a 1.2-star average, but ideally right at one star."

"I-I-I don't understand it," stammered Mary Hon. "I closely monitor the calls myself, and I am unaware of a single call that led to a satisfactory resolution. My team has been as unhelpful as Bacc'joonly possible. I frequently see them make the situation worse. Could it be that some of the customers have accidentally hit the wrong rating button? Could it be a survey interface problem?"

"If it was a survey interface problem, *Mary Hon*, then how come YOUR TEAM IS THE ONLY ONE ABOVE 1.2 STARS?" James Kon slapped the table and then broke down into further sobs. Mary Hon joined him.

Alice felt a primitive urge to leave and forget the whole mission. This much crying was not worth it. What a downer!

Vel appeared to share at least some of those sentiments, but when Alice looked at Caid, he was projecting tears in his eyes.

"We must proceed with caution," Dan whispered. "They appear to be emotionally volatile."

"Ya think?" replied Alice.

Unsure what further information she was waiting for, she stepped out into the doorway and approached the long committee table.

There were only four people around it, much smaller than the committee that used to make the decisions. While that was likely a boon for efficiency, she doubted the decisions coming out of this room were making the multiverse any safer than the non-decisions issued by the Jejoon leadership the last time she'd been there.

"Who are you?"

(Alice matched the voice to George Mon.)

Bracing her hands on her hips, Alice declared, "We're the Outer Space Outlaws!"

"Please," Caid said softly into her ear, "you're only hurting yourself with this."

"Are you from the Depot?" asked the Bacc'joon.

"We used to work for the Depot," said Alice, "but we don't anymore."

"Defectors!" James Kon shouted through his tears.

"All right, all right," said Alice, holding up her hands, "everyone calm the fuck down. We just want to talk to George Mon."

"About what?" George Mon asked.

"About the drilling."

The Bacc'joon wobbled agitatedly. "That is strictly confidential."

Alice's brows shot up. "Oh, is it? You mean these guys don't know about it?"

"Know about what?" said Mary Hon.

"Nothing," snapped George Mon. "Shut your mouth and focus on getting your customer satisfaction rating below the maximum."

Mary Hon's head drooped.

"You're telling me," said Alice, "that none of these people who are presumably Depot management know anything about the drilling at the edge of the universe?"

George Mon wobbled more furiously. "They don't need to know. They're not managers of expansion."

"Expansion?" asked James Kon. "Expansion of what?"

"Mind your business!"

"I will not!" He slapped the table but didn't break down into sobs this time.

"Please," said Dan, stepping forward. "We need your cooperation now more than ever."

"Why would we listen to a freak like you?" George Mon said, crinkling her knobby, lopsided nose at him. "What did the Depot crossbreed to create you, anyway?"

"The Depot didn't crossbreed anything," Dan said. "Pangolians are ancient people! Unlike Bacc'joons, which are true genetic fr—" Then he remembered and decided not to go there.

"Easy, boy," Alice murmured to him. "There might be an opportunity to beat their asses, but not yet."

"I'll have your back if that time comes," Vel muttered.

"Listen," said Alice, "I hate to bog down a party, but we've gotten a bit off track here. Can we get back to the drilling thing?"

"What about the drilling?" It was an older Bacc'joon who spoke. He'd thus far stayed out of the discussion, and the only signs of his age were that he looked slightly deflated, like a balloon two days after the party is over.

"The Depot is drilling at the edge of the universe," Alice explained. "They're risking everyone's life, the multiverse, and, well, *everything*, even the arrow of time, by doing it. My crew and I want to speak with whoever's in charge. We were told that would be you, George Mon."

She glared at Alice. "I'm in charge of some things, but I'm just a manager."

"Then who do you report to?"

"I report directly to the Depot."

"About that. Who, exactly?"

"No idea. It's the Depot."

Alice had heard this line before. It was the same one their liaison Liz Windsor had fed them when pressed. Alice could never put her finger on whether it was the truth or a script that Liz Windsor was forced to recite under penalty of something unpleasant.

"Well, uh, can you run it up the chain, then? Maybe suggest to whoever you report to that they stop the drilling because it could end us all?"

"We all die eventually," George Mon said.

"Nah, not like this. This is different, and I think you know that."

"There is no room for your cowardice in the face of expansion," said George Mon, "and expansion is the most important thing!"

"Is that so?" said Alice. "Explain it to me like I'm a child, then."

"Look at the sorry state of the multiverse," said George Mon.

James Kon muttered, "Terrible."

Mary Hon muttered, "Atrocious."

The older Bacc'joon remained silent.

"I dunno," said Alice. "I think it's great! Okay, maybe not that far, but it's *at least* fine."

"Intelligence leaves a trail of destruction and harm behind us wherever we go," George Mon said. "Don't lie to yourself. This multiverse is all used up, and so are we. Expansion gives us hope. Fresh places to explore, new frontiers. We're no longer stuck in the muck of our consequences."

James Mon looked on the verge of tears again as he said, "I killed both of my wives. I wish I hadn't. Every time I go home and look and my new wife, I think about the two I killed with a hammer. Void take me, how I wish I hadn't done that!"

"Um," said Alice.

But James Kon wasn't done. "This expansion, will it give me a fresh start?"

"Either that," said George Mon, "or it will erase everything, like this yellow-haired monster described."

James Kon nodded. "I could accept that. In fact, I would like it. I would like that very, very much."

"Uh," said Alice.

"I've killed a wife, too!" declared Mary Hon. "But that's not even the thing I wish most that I hadn't done. I cheated on her with another wife! For years! In front of her! I even had my second wife move in to help my first wife do her wifely duties of taking care of all my physical needs and emotional labor. My second wife, he hated the first, or so I thought. Then they started fucking! Behind my back, then in front of my face! I had to kill them both, but I only managed to kill my first wife. The second one escaped, and I've been searching for him in my spare time. I wish I had never taken the second wife. I wish I'd never had that affair so that I now spend every free moment seeking out my second wife to kill him instead of monitoring my team to make sure they're not rating too high in customer satisfaction!"

"Okay, but listen," said Alice. "Just hear me out. If the Depot pokes a hole into the wrong universe, *everything* you just described will be erased, not just the bad parts. All the good times you had with your wives will—"

"I had none of those," said Mary Hon. "I hated my wives."

"But you killed them for having sex in front of you?"

"Not for that! They should've been cooking me dinner and rubbing my feet! I want it all to go away! I want all these feelings to go away! I want everyone to be murdered and to never have existed!"

"Me too!" shouted James Kon.

"Now you're getting it," cheered George Mon. "Fresh markets or bust!" She pumped her weak fist into the air. "Fresh markets or bust!"

Then James Kon and Mary Hon joined her. "Fresh markets or bust!"

Alice turned to Vel. "At least they don't sound so miserable anymore."

"Oh no," said James Kon, "I still would very much like to die and be put out of my misery! I am a monstrosity! A crime against nature! I never should have been conceived!"

Vel said, "We could take them hostage. I could extract what I need from them."

"Could you?" Alice asked, staring with displeasure at the chanting table. "I wonder if they wouldn't enjoy the torture, though. They seem comfortable enough torturing themselves."

"May I?" Vel said.

Alice nodded for her to give it a whirl. "Threats but no murder."

"Have it your way." Vel pulled her blaster and shot it into the ceiling. It ended the obnoxious chant. "Nobody is leaving this room until we know how to get in contact with George Mon's Depot connections. I will pull you apart bit by bit if I have to. How do you think we found you all in the first place? Someone squealed. I have a way of making that happen. I'll… rip off your penises." She cringed at her lack of creativity. "And maybe do the same to your vulvas? Do you have vulvas?"

"Loosely speaking," said Mary Hon breathlessly.

Alice snickered.

"To be clear, it won't *all* be genital stuff," Vel explained, wondering how she'd gotten so off track. "It'll be other kinds of pain, too."

James Kon was grinning. "Will you kill us?"

"No," said Vel. "I'll do everything in my power to make sure you live a long and painful life."

James Kon let out an anguished cry, but it was cut short by someone else shouting.

"Tipgripper wank flunks!" Dan stuck a palm under his armpit and flapped his elbow like a wing until he nailed the farting sound.

"Void suck us in," said Vel, breaking from her threats to glare at him. "Right now?"

"Sorry."

"It's not his fault," said Alice. "He doesn't control the waves. Is it a big one, Dan?"

"Can't tell. It's slow coming in." He shivered, flapping his wrists. "Would you prefer I have a fit of the jitters? I can let it happen if that's less disruptive."

Vel sighed. "No."

Alice placed a steadying hand on his shoulder. "Of course not. No, we don't need you to go through that."

He slapped her in the face.

"Dammit!" She pressed a palm to the stinging skin. "That was right in my goddamn ear."

"Eat my junk, wife!"

Alice worked her jaw to fight off the sting. "What do you think, Susy?"

"It's time to call it. We can resume after the improbability wave passes. Not like we won't be able to find them again."

"You're leaving?" said Mary Hon, anxiously. "But I thought you were going to torture us. Please. I deserve it. And it'll make the sweet, sweet oblivion of the erasure even better."

Vel shoved Dan ahead of her to leave the committee room but stayed out of arm's reach to avoid taking one to the ear.

"Oh dear," Caid said to Alice. "I'm terribly worried about their hearts. They seem in such distress."

"You're probably right," said Alice, "which is why I'm so glad to be getting the hell out of here. Total bummers, all of them. Killing wives left and right..."

Dan tried to donkey-kick Vel as they emerged into the shade of the trees, and she calmly sidestepped his foot. "Maybe we can just grab up George Mon," she suggested. Dan lunged for her, and she pressed a palm to his forehead. He took swings at her torso but missed. "I bet I could extract the information we need."

"Tingle wits!" Dan slapped himself across the face.

Caid stared at his friend with concern. "You know I'm never one for control tactics, and I believe every body is sovereign, but perhaps we could consider acquiring some restraints for Dan while he's in this state."

Alice nodded. "I bet Allura has some bondage in her slot. We could set it up in—"

"Excuse me," came a meek voice behind her. She turned to find the old Bacc'joon staring up at her.

"Yes?"

"George Mon does not know who the Depot is. She does not know her contact. I know this to be true, because I also do not know who my Depot contact is. You are looking in the wrong place here."

"Great conversation, thanks. So helpful."

The old Bacc'joon missed the sarcasm completely and waved for Alice to lean in closer. "What you want is to find the *touchstone*."

"The what?"

"It will help you find the ones you're seeking. The ones at the top."

"And you know this, how?"

The deflated balloon grinned. "I overheard my supervisor's supervisor telling another supervisor about it. He referred to the touchstone. I found that interesting, so I looked into it."

"How did you do all of this?"

"I stayed silent," he said. "They don't expect you to stay silent. They thought I was senile. They talked."

Alice looked around, wondering distractedly what the fastest route back to the ship would be. Beside her, Vel had Dan's arms pinned behind his back, and he wasn't presently trying to break free. Instead, he was standing cross-eyed, trying to lick his own nose.

She returned her attention to the Bacc'joon. "Fine. Where do we find the touchstone? And what is it? And then what do we do? And why are you helping us?"

"One at a time." He pulled a strip of tree bark from his sleeve. On the inside of it were scribbled numbers. "Here are the coordinates. You will find the touchstone in this place."

"And what is it?"

"I do not know."

"You don't even know what it looks like?" Alice asked.

"No. And what it does is a mystery. But I overheard that it is nearly as old as the Depot itself and holds a strange connection with the Depot. If I wished to find those running the Depot, this is where I would go first."

Dan leaned forward between oddities and whispered, "This could be a trap."

"You're right," said Alice. She glared at the old man. "How do I know this is not a trap?"

"Why would I want to trap you?"

"I can think of countless reasons for that. Just answer my question. How do I know this is not a trap you're sending me and my crew straight into?"

"You don't." He grinned. "But what are your options?"

The guy had a point, and even Dan was forced to concede to the pragmatism of it. He did so with a restrained curtsy.

"Why help us?" Alice asked. "Don't you have a bunch of things you wish you didn't do that you want to erase?"

"Oh, I've killed some wives." He chuckled, which turned into a dry cough. "Some I wish I hadn't killed, some I'm glad I did. There is much I've done that I wish I had not done. Speaking to you now might make the list later. I have many, many things I wish could be wiped clean from the arrow of time."

"Then *why* are you helping us?"

"Because not everyone will make the same decisions I have. Thinking about what I wish I had not done makes me imagine a version of me who has not done those things. Perhaps he is happy. I wish for others to have the opportunity to be happy, even though I am not and never will be. That cannot happen if the multiverse is destroyed."

Alice looked down at the piece of bark in her hand. The coordinates were legible, but only just. "All right. Screw it. We'll do our best." She considered offering her hand to shake, but then remembered the way Bacc'joon hands looked with their weird, bendy fingers and rough, cracked palms with the ooze. Instead, she said, "What's your name?"

"Bon Bon."

"Ah." She sucked the inside of her cheek to keep from saying what she wanted to say. "Great to meet you, Bon Bon. Thank you."

Dan performed a mix between the jitterbug and twerking as he boarded the ship a few minutes later.

"You two," said Alice, once Vel had dragged the hostages out of Caid's room. "Get the hell out of here."

"We home?" said Gool Don. "We on Bacc'joonia?"

"Goddamn," muttered Alice. "For a minute there I forgot y'all ruined Bacc'nalia. No, we're not there. We're on Location, remember? That's where George Mon is. You… Never mind. No. You'll be fine here, though. Get off and go start over." And as the glass elevator doors closed behind them, she called, "And for all that's holy, don't agree to be anyone's wife!"

CHAPTER
TWELVE

Dan retreated to his cabin almost immediately. Nobody blamed him for wanting to be weird in peace, though Alice did wonder if wanting to be alone with his weirdness might now be predictable for him and therefore thwarting his attempts to stave off the jitters.

Then again, she hardly understood how any of that worked, so she trusted him to do what he needed to do.

"Perhaps it'd be better to stay on the ground," said Vel, standing next to the navigator's chair.

Alice paced the bridge. "Does it matter? If we stay here to ride out the wave, improbable things will happen. Maybe we'll end up in space against our will. That would be improbable. Or maybe we'll be hit by a meteor!"

"Meteorite," Vel corrected her, "and we could experience a similar impact in space, depending on how strong the improbability is."

"You're right. But if we go into space, we could end up in some sort of… space fold loop where we speed through eternity forever, unable to escape."

"That would be improbable," Vel conceded.

"Are you open to receiving feedback?" Caid asked from where he stared out the front window onto the thick Location forest.

"Sure."

He turned to Alice. "I'm observing your pacing, and it makes me wonder if you're stuck in an anxiety spiral."

Alice rolled her eyes. "You're thinking of Dan. I don't have anxiety."

"Mmm..." Caid said.

Alice waited for more, but it didn't come. "What?"

"I believe you and I have different definitions of the word *anxiety*. Sometimes looking for an escape route is a form of anxiety."

Alice held up her hands. "Okay, you got me. I'm a little bit anxious. Can you blame me? Have you been following along with *anything* that's happened in the last few chapters?"

Caid's brows pinched together. "Chapters?"

Alice blinked and paused in her pacing. "I don't know why I said that. I meant hours. Obviously."

"It's a strange slip to make," said Vel. "We might be in a stronger wave than we even thought." She went to check the ship's controls, which were lighting up in such a way that they would've synced perfectly to the 1980 hit song by Queen "Another One Bites the Dust," but Vel couldn't know that, so it went unnoticed by all.

"So, yeah, I'm a little anxious," Alice said. "You gonna tell me to take a deep breath? You think that'll help me?"

"I think so," Caid replied, "but I know better than to suggest it to you right now."

"Oh." Alice let her guard down slightly. "Okay. Then what was your suggestion for me?"

"I was going to suggest that, because you seem

trapped in your mind, perhaps now would be a good time to tap into your heart and see what it has to say about the situation."

"Great idea. Allura? Could you, like, run some calculations for me that take into consideration the intensity and duration of the upcoming improbability wave, the probabilities of success on our ultimate mission if we stay on Location during it or leave the planet, and let me know what we should do?"

"Yes, Daddy. Mmm… grinding those numbers."

Caid gave up and returned to staring out the window. Advice, no matter how wise, was only useful when the person who needed it was ready to receive it. That was clearly not the case here.

"A most improbable thing just happened, Daddy."

Alice thought she might already know, but asked, "What is it?" anyway.

"The calculations show that the probability of success for both staying and leaving under these conditions is identical, down to the one hundredth decimal point."

"What about the one hundred and first, then?" Alice asked, crossing her fingers.

"Leaving the planet has a slight advantage."

Alice threw her hands in the air. "And we have a winner! Susy? Take us up!"

Opting for his reverie, Caid decided not to mention how improbable it would be for Allura to blatantly lie about the math. Highly improbable. Or, perhaps, just improbable enough.

"The coordinates take us to Morgan VFP2121," Allura explained.

They'd been in flight for nearly an hour, cruising through the improbability wave with nothing more improbable happening than Caid turning briefly into a pitchfork with wings. Within the last ten minutes, Dan had poked his head out onto a bridge twice, surveying the scene. Or maybe he was still attempting to be unpredictable.

"Morgan VFP2121 is locally known as Putterpantsia. The planet is home to extreme biological diversity, despite having been colonized by the Depot approximately four hundred local years ago."

"Wait," said Alice. "Colonized by the Depot? Not, like, by Homo sapiens, right?"

"Correct."

"Is it still a Depot stronghold?" Vel asked.

"It is still listed on the Depot's registry of friendly planets."

"What does that mean, exactly?" asked Alice.

Vel provided the explanation. "The Depot includes on its 'friendly planets' registry any planet where it's made its mark and feels like it has a significant amount of influence. Doesn't tell us much about how strong a physical presence the Depot has there, though."

"What else can you tell us about Putterpantsia, Allura?" asked Alice.

"It is known within its solar system as being a planet largely inhabited by self-identified artists and creatives."

"Oh no," said Alice and Vel together.

But Caid, who had been playing a holographic game of solitaire at the kitchenette table, perked up. "How energizing!"

"Wrong," said Alice. "I'd like to think I know a thing or two about what's energizing. Coffee? Yes. Adrenaline? Yes. Cocaine? Depends on what you mix it with. But artists?" She shook her head. "I had a real hard-on for them in college. God only knows why. I can say with certainty that no matter how sane of a person you believe yourself to be, you *will* reach a breaking point giving hand jobs to Fellini films."

"I hear the meaning in your words, and I value your experience," said Caid.

"Susy doesn't like artists, either. Do you, Susy?"

"No," said Vel. "I've not had great experiences with artists in the past. My brother was murdered by a roving band of artists. His blood was used to paint the walls of their colony, and as of the time I left Blerg VFP69, traces of his entrails can be found in at least one painting in every gallery around the globe."

"Wow. That definitely beats the hand job thing," said Alice.

Caid pressed his palms to his heart. "I receive your experience and pain, Vel. I am so sorry that happened to you. My experiences with fellow artists have been spiritually uplifting, and I hope that both of you will be able to receive my truth the way I've received yours."

Alice didn't miss the "fellow." Figured. Every sensitive guy she'd ever met considered himself an artist, whether he produced anything or not. One dude in her dorm called himself a "pizza artist" because he brought his own parmesan cheese to the dining hall and took way too long sprinkling it over his greaseball slice just the way he wanted it.

"You're sure those are the coordinates, Allura?" Alice asked. "An *artsy* planet?"

"That is where the coordinates you gave me point to, Daddy."

"Maybe there's some mistake," Alice said hopefully. "Maybe this is just, like, the place where we find the next coordinates for the *real* place where we can find the touchstone. Ooh! Maybe they'll have the real coordinates spelled out on the planet's surface in big boulders!"

Just then, Dan shuffled onto the bridge, and the conversation came to a halt, while everyone watched to see what strange thing he might be about to do.

"Don't worry," he said before slumping into the gunner's seat, "I'm feeling better. Just please *don't* do anything improbable right now. I need a rest."

"The wave passed?" Alice asked.

"For now. It might just be a temporary trough, but I'll take what I can get."

The Pangolian had dark circles under his almond eyes, which he could hardly keep open. All that boogieing really took it out of him.

Vel brought over a mug of coffee that had been brewing at the kitchenette specifically for Dan's eventual recovery. He clutched it between his hands like it was fruit from the tree of life. "What did I miss?"

"We're going to an artsy planet to find the touchstone," said Alice.

He stared morosely into the dark surface of his mug. "Fuck."

Alice grinned proudly. "Don't worry, Susy and I aren't big on it either."

"I'm sensing that this stop, while likely crucial to our mission," said Caid, "will provide a beautiful opportunity for each one of us to witness parts of our true essence and reconnect with our inner child."

"I'll opt out of that, if I can," said Dan.

Caid nodded sympathetically. "You must be very tired. Perhaps you can stay here and rest."

"Oh no, it's not that. It's just that my inner child was bullied horribly at school. I had to put the little guy down."

Vel chuckled.

"Oh," said Caid, "how my heart weeps for the young Danger Zone who was not properly protected."

Dan, feeling an uncomfortable sensation creep into his body, decided to change the subject. "What exactly is the plan here, Alice? Or should I even ask that?"

"Actually," she said, grinning, "I have a semblance of a whole plan in mind, not just the first step."

"You're getting better at this," said Dan. "I was worried you wouldn't, but you are."

"Thank you. Here's what we do. We go to this freaky-ass artist planet and find the touchstone, whatever that is. If it's small enough to move, then we take it with us and get the hell outta there."

"I like it already," said Vel.

"And then we use the touchstone to track down the people running the Depot. I'm sick of them hiding behind anonymity. I want to pull off those gosh-darn masks and reveal who they are to the entire multiverse. Maybe even get some justice out of it."

"That might be hoping for too much," advised Dan, "but go on. What then?"

"Then, uh, we'll take down the Depot, obviously."

Dan's mouth fell open. Alice didn't like that. She turned to see if Vel was similarly stunned, but only found the woman grimacing. Finally, Alice looked at Caid for a response.

"Hmm…" he said, ambiguously. "Hmm…"

"What is it?" she demanded. "What's everyone all worried about? I thought it kind of went without saying that this is what we've been hoping to do this whole time. Isn't that what the Alliance has been trying to do from the start? Take down the Depot? And if we can find the touchstone, we might actually have a shot at it."

"I don't know about that," said Dan. "Don't know about it at all."

"Which part?"

"The part of your plan where we take down the Depot."

"Cut off the head of the snake!" Alice chopped the air.

Dan wiped a hand down his face. "Vel, could you explain why this is a terrible idea?"

"Nope. It's all you, Dan."

"Ugh. Fine. It's a good *idea*, Alice, but doing what you propose would kill billions, if not trillions, of intelligent lifeforms. It would starve entire planets."

She squinted at him. "That sounds not good. Explain, please."

"Let's just say that we somehow manage to stop the drilling, right? Maybe we find the people in charge and Vel tortures them into giving the orders from the top down to end the practice at all their stations. Assuming the word is competently conveyed, and the project is halted, killing the ones running the Depot would quickly halt *all* operations as instructions stop coming down from the top."

"Isn't that what everyone wants? No more drilling. No more third-party selling. No more monopoly."

"Not everyone," said Vel. "If *everyone* wanted it, the Depot never would've gotten as large as it is."

"By some estimates, nearly half of the interplanetary infrastructure in our multiverse is maintained and run by the Depot," Dan said. "And remember the marketplace on Vongarian? Most marketplaces are just like that. There are even entire planets whose enforcement and regulatory bodies are staffed entirely by people devoted to the Depot. Not only is it unlikely that cutting off the head of the snake would make them change a single thing about the way they operate, but it would be disastrous if it did."

"Okay, so it's a messy process," said Alice, "but it'll return the decisions back to the planets. And those third-party sellers can become first-party sellers."

"They're third-party sellers, Alice!" Dan said. "They don't know how to build a platform! You can't just tell them to sell direct and expect them to know how! Businesses will crumble. Groups will starve. It's not just messy; at best, it's chaos."

"And out of chaos," Vel added, "someone else will appear. Maybe they're more benevolent than the Depot, but maybe they're even more malignant. The Depot has expertly cultivated a public image of being benevolent and putting the good of the consumer first. People like that message. They think, *Hey! I'm a consumer! They have my best interest in mind!* But then they fail to remember they are also the seller. The seller who shares profit with a middleman that adds no value but 'visibility,' because they have taken over every visible space. And they're also the workers. The ones who aren't paid fairly and have no options of other places to toil away their days."

Alice grasped the sides of her head, battling a headache that was setting in rapidly. "And the mass casualties are from...?"

"Imagine if all your bones were replaced by lead bones," said Dan.

"I'd rather not."

"And now imagine someone can melt down the lead bones and drain them from you. How well do you think your body would hold together?"

"Reckon I'd look a little like a Kaldalk. Without the weird horn, obviously. Or do I have a weird horn in this metaphor?"

"Alice," said Vel, "for better or worse—definitely worse—the Depot is essential to the function of the multiverse. Commerce depends on it now. If you take out the Depot, you take out most of commerce, and that means starvation, unsafe working conditions, narrowing the market for many sellers."

"I cannot stress enough," said Dan, "how woefully unprepared third-party sellers are to sell direct to customers."

"Things might right themselves over time," Vel continued, "but during that adjustment period, trillions could die."

"Y'all got me all frazzled and turned around," Alice said. "First, you're like, 'Let's kill all the workers at the drilling stations,' and now you're warning me against doing something that would cause mass casualties."

"I'm not warning you against it," Vel said. "I'm telling you what would happen. You can do whatever you want with that information. Frankly, I'm not concerned about it. Billions of life forms have expired around the multiverse during the course of this conversation. You can't stop death, which is why it doesn't bother me. Erasure is the only thing I'm concerned about."

"That's bleak," said Dan.

Vel shrugged but didn't disagree.

"Does Leviathan want to see the Depot fall?" Alice asked.

"Dunno," said Dan, "you'd have to ask her."

"Allura, would you ring Leviathan?"

"Yes, Daddy."

The viewing window at the front of the bridge turned opaque, and Vel's face plus a scar filled the screen.

"Alice," said President Leviathan promptly, "we were wondering when you and your crew would check in. I see you were on Location. Any particular reason for that?"

"First of all, tracking people without their knowledge is creepy. Secondly, we were on Location because I've decided there's no way we're ever going to recruit enough Alliance members to convince the drillers to stop drilling. We're going up the ladder."

Leviathan didn't appear especially impressed. "You know, if you'd run that by me, I would have told you that we'd already tried it."

"Huh?"

"One of our scouts tracked communication from a drilling site back to a Bacc'joon named George Mon at Location."

"You shitting me? Was that scout successful getting anything out of George Mon?"

"No."

"Ha!"

"Were you?"

"Well, no."

"Are you returning to headquarters, then?" asked Leviathan.

"Nope. We have somewhere better we're already en route to."

"And that is?"

"You'll find out once we land, won't you? You clearly installed tracking software on this thing before handing it over. We shoulda guessed. No free lunches, I reckon. But that's not why I called. I called because I got a question for you." She made Leviathan wait as payback for tracking them, then said, "If you had a chance to take down the Depot at the top, would you?"

Alice caught only the smallest eyebrow raise on Leviathan's face. "Absolutely."

"But don't you think it would cause mass casualties when the infrastructure or whatever collapsed?"

"I do believe that."

"And you would do it anyway?"

"There are mass casualty events taking place in the multiverse nearly every moment, none of which my actions have anything to do with. If I were to play a part in but one of them, that would be a small price for my conscience to pay to know that I'd removed the overreach of the Depot and allowed space for the small business of the multiverse to rebuild from the ashes."

"You're supposing," said Dan, "that another entity just like the Depot wouldn't come along and fill the vacuum before everyone could rebuild individually."

Leviathan glared at him through the screen. "You don't approve?"

Before Dan could respond, Alice said, "Hell no, we don't approve being a part of a mass casualty event if there's any other option."

"They happen regularly," Leviathan said. "You've already been a part of one—why not a second?"

"Hold your horses there, Susy 2.0. I didn't participate in no goddamn mass murder."

Dan eyed his captain with caution. Double negatives were usually a sign that she was getting worked up. He'd have to keep an eye on her.

"But you have," Leviathan persisted. "The Bacc'joons are a scourge upon the multiverse, but particularly upon Location and what was formerly Bacc'nalia."

"I agree they're nasty and nightmarish, but mass casualties? C'mon, Lev."

"You haven't read the updated history logs, clearly."

Alice looked to Dan and Vel, who both shook their heads. She didn't bother looking at Caid; he only ever read vibes. "We've been a little busy as of late. Maybe you can, uh, give us a summary."

"Certainly. The Bacc'nalians and Jejoons combined their populations for the period of one generation. The babies were so ugly that it almost halted crossbreeding practices immediately. However, the parents held out hope that things would turn a corner once puberty hit. But things only got worse when that happened. And then they worsened still upon reaching the age of full maturity. The Bacc'joons had neither the adventurous and spontaneous spirit of the Bacc'nalians nor the caution and thoughtfulness of the Jejoons. Instead, the Bacc'joons were found to be needlessly reckless in tedious ways. The breeding between the two groups stopped after the first forty years. It was labeled a failed experiment, and both populations attempted to return to the way things were— Bacc'nalians mating with Bacc'nalians, and Jejoons not mating with Jejoons or anyone else, really."

"I think I see where this is going," Alice said. "Both populations dwindled over time, and the Bacc'joons took over the planets."

"Wrong. The Bacc'joon population was not particularly

large or genetically diverse, but it was sexually active. Extremely sexually active. And essentially left to its own devices. Through both inbreeding and neglect from ill-equipped parents, the population's intelligence suffered. Finally, it reached the Crimson Limit."

Dan gulped.

"What's that?" Alice asked. "What's the Crimson Limit?"

"It's the point at which a species' average social intelligence dips too low to include compassion and forethought and is just high enough to survive as a species."

"What happens then?" Alice was almost afraid to ask.

"When a population hits the Crimson Limit, it reaches its point of highest violence. This almost inevitably leads to genocide of other species."

"Ruh-roh," muttered Alice. "You're telling me that the Bacc'nalis and Jejoons didn't, ya know, just die off slowly?"

"Oh, they died off," said Leviathan, "and sometimes it was a slow death."

"I'm not saying you're wrong," said Vel, "but we saw living Jejoons on Location while we were there."

"There is a surviving colony of them, yes. It seems that a small number were able to hide away until the Bacc'joons finally devolved below the Crimson Limit. And while it's hardly a consolation, the threat the Jejoons were living under and the trauma from seeing their families slaughtered was, it seems, enough to kick-start their libido. That's why the small population of Jejoons on Location has been able to sustain itself."

"Happily ever after," said Dan, sipping his coffee and finding it unpleasantly room temperature.

"I don't tell you about the tragic history to hurt you," Leviathan said. "I mention it only to show you that you do not have clean hands here, Alice. None of you do. To stop doing what needs to be done now because you're worried your conscience might not be up to the task of knowing you have death on your hands is impractical at best, actively harmful at worst. You already have the stain of those slaughtered Bacc'nalis and Jejoons on you, so what's one more mass casualty event, especially if it's one that could prevent future mass casualty events?"

Alice thought it over. "Cool, cool. Great talk, Lev. If I didn't know better, I'd guess Lev is short for Levity, because this has been an absolute pleasure. Chat soon." She hit the button to end the call, and in the silence on the bridge that followed, she helped herself to a cup of coffee as well, pouring it slowly, hoping she could strike the perfect spot of caffeination where she felt slightly optimistic again but wasn't so invigorated that her mind went to the topics she was hoping to ignore for a while longer.

She turned and faced the crew, leaning against the end of the kitchenette table. "Welp."

"Wish I could unhear *all* of that," said Dan.

"Even I'm a little upset about it," added Vel, "and I've slaughtered hundreds with my bare hands."

"It's almost too much to think about," said Caid. "And I feel more convinced than ever that this visit to the artist's colony is exactly what our souls are crying out for. Through art, we can find all kinds of ways to process this traumatic information. Sometimes the best thing for an overburdened conscience is a deep experience of creativity."

Dan looked at Vel and Alice. "Are we still heading to Putterpantsia, knowing what we know? What's the plan?"

Alice chuckled. "The plan? I have no idea. But one thing I will tell you is we're finding the touchstone, and then—"

The ship lurched, and Allura said, "Shitballs."

Alice yelped as scalding coffee splashed onto her hand. "Ach!" She chucked the coffee cup across the bridge before her brain could catch up.

Alarms clanged and lights flashed menacingly on the control panels.

The lights would've matched up perfectly to "Steal My Sunshine" by the one-hit wonder Len, if anybody had bothered to play it at that very moment.

"What's happening?" demanded Vel, anchoring herself in the navigator's seat and scanning the panels for clues.

Dan provided the answer, albeit indirectly: "Noodlehog! Knock-knock!"

"Who's there?" replied Alice. The ship lurched again, and she was forced to grab for the countertop to keep from being tossed around.

With a pop that was drowned out by the alarm systems, Caid turned into a keg of IPA with a mouth. "This might be the biggest improbability wave we've encountered," he said. "Let's not become disconnected from our true nature as we hold on."

"Don't lecture us about true nature," snapped Alice, losing her grip on the counter as the ship tipped and sliding sideways on her ass across the bridge, "when you're a goddamn keg!"

Alice got her feet under her enough to crawl to the captain's chair and buckle in.

"What are you seeing, Dan?" asked Vel.

He turned his head side to side as he monitored the situation through the gunner's helmet. "No enemy crafts that I can see. I don't believe we're being fired at. Baldop! Zingerflamadoo!" He threw the rest of his cold coffee onto his lap when another wave of jitters threatened to spread from the center of his spine.

Through the viewing window, the stars spun in a tighter and tighter circle.

Alice's stomach hadn't felt like this since her sophomore year of high school when she'd set a speed record among her friends for Edward Fortyhands and then jumped on the Tilt-a-Whirl at the traveling carnival.

"How much—" She snapped her mouth shut as the puke invaded it. She swallowed it down. "How much more on this wave? Any inkling, Dan?"

"Go fuck yourself."

"Susy? Any—" She swallowed it down again.

"No idea. But if this doesn't end soon, we could end up horribly off track. I see a space fold up ahead that isn't logged on any of our maps. I have no idea where it might dump us out or how much time we'll lose when we cross through."

Vel hit the manual steering override, and the wheel popped out. She gripped it so tightly that she ran the risk, under these conditions, of the particles in her hands passing straight between the particles of the wheel. She turned it all the way in the opposite direction of the intense spin, which did nothing to make Alice less likely to puke on herself.

"Almost stabilized," said Vel.

She was so focused on counteracting the spin that she almost overlooked the more important problem they now faced: the uncharted space fold.

It had the usual appearance of a space fold that the crew had come to expect—a slightly wobbly appearance, transparent, the occasional burst of light slipping through from the other side—but this one had another feature that none of them had not seen before. Instead of being roughly circular, it was shaped like the letter H.

"Watch it, Susy!" Alice yelled, as they hurled straight for the space fold's connecting line.

"I'm trying!" She jerked the steering column to nosedive and avoid the oncoming fold, but there was a slight problem: her wheel had turned into a framed cross-stitch of a mouse playing checkers with a parrot. She blinked at it. "Oh. Um." She held up the cross-stitch for Alice to see. The women locked eyes. Both sighed.

And into the uncharted space fold they went, Vel gripping the cross-stitch, Alice's hands still stinging from the scalding coffee, Dan doing the hand jive while shouting gibberish, and Caid simply being a keg of IPA.

CHAPTER
THIRTEEN

The ship hurtled into the space fold.

Suddenly, the alarms fell silent. The lights stopped flashing. Dan stopped dancing. Vel was no longer holding a cross-stitch. Caid resembled an IPA enthusiast rather than a keg of the drink itself.

The space fold spat them out with such force that there was no stopping the ship as it burst through the atmosphere of the nearby planet.

Flames danced around the edges of the windshield as charged particles collided with it.

Vel yanked on the steering wheel, and the ship decelerated as they passed through the outermost layers of the alien atmosphere and land came into view below them.

Alice only had a moment to admire the green and blue before said green was rushing toward them much faster than she would've liked.

"Good news and bad news," said Vel.

"Bad news first!" Alice shouted, bracing.

"We're going to crash-land. Too much velocity. I can't counteract it."

"Good news?"

"It shouldn't be so violent that we all die instantaneously."

"What about slowly?" Dan asked.

"That depends on whether we can survive outside our ship and whether we can ever get this thing back off the ground again."

"Great," said Dan.

"Hey!" said Alice. "You're feeling better!"

Dan braced for impact. "Nope. Just feeling a different kind of bad."

"Everyone strapped in?" asked Vel.

"Check," said Dan.

"Roger that," said Alice.

"I'm firmly grounded," said Caid, his palms pressed together.

The ship plowed into the ground at an angle and skipped like a rock.

Each time it did, a wash of reddish dirt filled the window, and Alice felt like her head was about to pop off her body.

Finally, they skidded to a halt, and the bridge fell silent, as those on it ran a quick check on their internal and external organs.

Dan leaned to the side and vomited.

"Ship diagnostics, Allura?"

"Everything appears to be intact, Big Susy, apart from the graviton dampener."

Vel grunted. "Then we're stuck, aren't we?"

"Only until the dampener is repaired. Would you like

me to open up my engine hood and let you poke around inside?"

Vel sighed. "I wouldn't even know where to start with a graviton dampener."

Alice stared ahead at the bland landscape. Shapes not too unlike cacti rose from the dusty plane ahead of them. "Allura, any intel on what this planet is?"

"No, Daddy. It does not exist in my database."

Alice looked at Dan. "Are we through the improbability wave yet?"

He nodded weakly. His pearlescent skin lacked its normal luster.

Vel scanned the control panel in front of her. "Are these numbers accurate?"

"Yes, Big Susy."

Vel turned to the others. "Atmosphere appears to be within a safe range for us, and there are heat signals compatible with life only a few miles off. Maybe someone here has what we need to get back in the sky again."

Alice unbuckled herself and rolled her head to stretch out her sore neck. "Let's do it, then."

"We'll need coats. The temperature is 270 degrees."

"Damn, Susy! Since when is that coat weather?"

"Kelvin," Vel replied. "That's cold."

"Ah. I mean, obviously."

"It converts to about twenty-six degrees Fahrenheit."

"Jumping Jesus! This place trying to kill me?"

"It might be," said Dan, pushing himself out of his chair with some effort, "and not just through the cold. We have no idea what is waiting for us out there. Are the local intelligent life forms half our size? Ten times it? Are they symmetrical? Sentient?" He shook his head. "If the cold doesn't kill you, something else might."

"Allura," said Alice. "Could you get Dan *both* of his daily boosters? He's being a bummer."

"I already had one of them," said Dan.

"Two boosters coming up," said Allura.

Alice froze. She looked at Dan, who appeared confused, then she looked at Vel, who was visibly concerned.

"Why are you shaking your head like that, Susy?" said Alice, grinning.

"Just because the Depot restriction on boosters has been lifted does *not* mean it's suddenly a better idea to have more than two a day."

Alice smirked. "We'll see about that. We will see about that." She grabbed the boosters from the nearest slot and handed them to Dan. "Pop 'em."

He threw back the boosters, and his luster began returning immediately.

Alice held up her hands when she saw that Vel was still glaring at her. "I won't do a bunch of boosters before we explore an alien planet we know nothing about, okay? Sheesh. Give me a little credit. *He's* the one who huffed Hypha. If anyone around here has a problem, it's him."

As they loaded onto the elevator to descend into the loading dock, Alice said, "Oh, wait! I forgot something," and jumped off as the door closed. She pretended to head toward her cabin until the lift was out of sight, and then she stopped at the nearest slot and grabbed two boosters, popping one right away.

When she met them in the lower deck, they were already slipping on large fur coats. Alice had worried that the coats they'd worn during Vel's kidnapping rescue would only be available through the Depot, but it looked like pimp coats were standard multiversal wear.

"What'd you forget?" Vel asked, eyeing Alice closely.

"Craziest thing. I thought I forgot my boots, but then I realized I was already wearing them."

Vel rolled her eyes, and they waited until everyone was warmly dressed and armed to the teeth with blasters before lowering the port.

The cold air immediately swirled its way beneath the bottom of Alice's coat and nipped at her legs through the jumpsuit.

Dan, however, didn't mind the cold. He usually ran hot beneath his thick, armored skin, and thanks to the boosters, he felt revitalized. He was the first to step out of the ship and plant a foot on the new planet. Sure, he had no idea what was in store for him, but he could probably handle it. They all could. They'd faced strange things together before.

He inhaled the cold air and let it fill his lungs. Perhaps another improbability wave wouldn't pass them for a while. Perhaps they would get a little lucky!

But wait, what if it was so improbable for a wave to *not* show up while they were here that by it not arriving, it would send him into jitters?

Alice thumped him on the back just in time to knock his brain off track. "Not the prettiest planet, but at least the air works for us, right? I guess we should find some intelligent life forms if we stand a chance of getting the parts we need."

"There," said Dan, pointing toward the horizon.

Alice squinted but saw nothing. "I don't see anything."

"You don't?"

"Aw hell, this isn't a ghasselite situation again, is it?"

"I hope not," said Dan. "Regardless, I see some sort of structure this way, and there's smoke coming from it."

Alice squinted again. "Oh! I do see the smoke. Wow, way to pick that out. Let's go."

Only a few minutes of trekking across the dry, bumpy ground brought the structure close enough that everyone could see it plainly. A small cabin. Not on fire, but with smoke issuing from the chimney. Vel held out an arm, telling the crew to hold where they were once the cabin was still a hundred yards off. "We have no idea who or what might be in there. There's a good chance we'll be met with hostility. I recommend we send Caid first."

"Smart," said Dan.

The hologram nodded. "I think that's an excellent plan built on concern and compassion for your friends. The caution seems most warranted and not a result of past trauma."

"I'm sure it's both," said Vel. "But either way..." She nodded for him to go on ahead.

"Hold up," said Alice. "If whoever lives there asks who we are, tell them we go by the name—"

"I'm sorry," said Caid, shaking his head slowly. "I will not."

They waited, crouching low, as Caid approached the cabin. Unable to knock, he hollered for whomever or whatever might be inside.

The door opened, but they couldn't see past Caid to view the inhabitant.

No shots were fired. That was something.

Caid continued conversing with whomever or whatever, and as a bitter wind blew their way, the rest of the crew was able to catch snippets of muddled voices. Alice swore she heard a chuckle.

Finally, Caid turned around and waved them over.

Alice was the last one to file into the warm cabin, and

it took her eyes a moment to adjust to the darkness after the bright sunlight reflecting off the shimmering dirt. The savory smell of roasting meat hit her immediately, and her eyes moved to the fire in the fireplace. Something dead was skewered on a spit over the flames, its skin beginning to crackle.

"Friends," said Caid. "Let me introduce you to our gracious new friend, who's kindly allowed us to warm up in his home. This is Tucker."

Still staring at the fire, Alice blinked and pulled her attention toward the host, saying, "For real? I used to date a guy named Tuck—"

The fuck? This made no sense, though. Her pupils must be malfunctioning from staring at the flames. She blinked a few more times.

No. Still him.

On an uncharted planet, in a mysterious part of the multiverse, endless light-years away from Blerg VFP69, Alice found herself staring into the unmistakable adult face of her seventh-grade sweetheart, Tucker King.

CHAPTER
FOURTEEN

"That can't be you," she said.

Tucker was dressed in bland, dirty clothes that he might've sewn himself. A thick black fur hung around his shoulders—nothing she'd ever seen him wear before. But maybe they didn't have Aeropostale on this planet. Yeah, probably not.

His expression as he stared at her with his deep brown eyes was unreadable. Was that a glimmer of recognition in his pupils, or only a reflection of the dancing flames?

Finally, he said, "Can't be who?"

"Tucker King."

"Oh. No, I'm not Tucker King. I'm Tucker Blonkonuk."

Alice squinted at him. "You sure about that?"

"Yes."

Vel looked from Alice to the host, trying to piece it together. The name Tucker King rang the gentlest of bells in her memory, but she couldn't place it. It was no secret to anyone that Alice still had massive gaps in her understanding of how space travel worked, but why would she believe that she knew someone on a planet this distant? Surely, she understood the odds of that were so low as to be negligi—

Vel's mouth fell open. Tucker King. Alice had talked about him before. Someone she'd known on Earth.

"Okey-dokey," said Alice. "If you say so." She winked at him.

Tucker pressed his lips together and cocked his head to the side. "I'm serious."

"I believe you," she said, flashing a smile that didn't reach anywhere near her eyes. She gave him a thumbs-up.

While Dan wasn't versed in the culture on this mysterious planet, he knew confusion when he saw it, and the body language of their host screamed it. "Where are we?" Dan asked.

"In my cabin."

"And where is your cabin?"

"Outside town."

"Excellent," said Dan. "Thanks. No more information needed."

"Are you hungry?" Tucker nodded toward the fire. "It's not much, but I have more hanging out back I can make for myself."

"Mmm," said Alice, "almost looks as good as a Santa Fe Gordita Crunch!" She eyed Tucker's expression closely, but there was no reaction to the shared reference.

Huh, strange. Maybe he *was* telling the truth. Maybe he wasn't the same Tucker King she farted in front of at the seventh-grade dance because she'd eaten too much Taco Bell beforehand. He'd handled it about as well as a boy that age could, considering a girl he liked farting in front of him was about the most mind-altering event he could've encountered.

Long after she'd broken up with Tucker King, they

remained friends. That was how it had to be in a small town like Slip'n'Fall, Texas. You cycled through all forms of relationship with the same twenty people in your class from kindergarten through high school graduation. And if you were lucky, some of them moved away and others arrived every few years.

One night, years after the middle school dance incident, she'd shared a bottle of whisky with Tucker by the Boyds' bonfire and confided in him about the culprit, the Gordita Crunch. He'd laughed until he nearly passed out.

There was no way Tucker wouldn't remember that. And yet this one seemed clueless.

Of course it's not the same Tucker, she chided herself. *Tucker King is long dead back on Earth. His bones have turned to dust.*

She swallowed hard and decided to move on from the inquiry.

The thing on the spit could've been a large rat as easily as a small opossum, but of course it was neither. It was a thing called a Bobber'y, which was meaner than a cornered opossum and carried more diseases than a rat.

Tucker didn't warn them about that as they ate, and it was just as well; none of the diseases passed along by the Bobber'y were very interesting. One slightly shifted your perception of the color periwinkle so that your brain read it as lavender, another decreased the sensitivity of tastebuds by 0.05%, and so forth.

Bobber'ys were not generally revered for their taste anyway. They tasted like the bottom of a work boot. In fact, while no one would be expected to know this, the Bobber'y tasted *worse* than the bottom of Alice's Texas-flag boots.

"Mmm," said Dan, moving the burned meat to the

back of his mouth so his molars could take a stab at it. They had no more luck getting through the tough fibers than his sharper teeth, though. "Thank you for your generosity, Tucker."

"Caid said your ship crashed nearby. You're looking for someone with mechanical know-how and a part."

"That's right," said Alice, and when Tucker turned toward her, Dan took the opportunity to spit out his meat and hide it on his coat pocket. "We're under a bit of a time crunch to get out of here. We were trying to get to a completely different planet, but, well, shit went south."

"Shit went south," Tucker said. "Never heard that phrase before, but I can guess what it means. And I like it." He smiled at her, and her heart skipped a beat.

Why had she ended it with Tucker? She couldn't even remember. But that smile. She sure did remember that.

"You'll want to head on into town for the right kinda help," he said. "It's a bit of a ways on, though, so I'll lend you a couple of horses to speed things up, if you're interested."

"Horses?" Alice asked.

"You'd do that?" said Vel. "How do you know we won't steal your horses?"

Tucker shrugged. "I hope you won't. But them girls are trained well. You leave 'em untied once, and they'll find their way back." He paused. "I suppose it sounds a little reckless of me to offer, but for whatever reason, I trust you. I trusted Caid the moment I saw him, and you"—he wagged a finger at Alice—"you remind me of someone, and I can't quite figure who, but it gives me a good feeling."

"We'll bring the horses back," Alice assured him. "No matter what. We won't skip town with them."

Alice and Vel were only just starting to make headway on the Bobber'y meat they'd been futilely masticating when Tucker led them outside and toward the stables. Both women spat out the meat as soon as they had the chance, but the bitter taste of burned rubber lingered.

Tucker opened the barn gate and whistled. Four beasts very close to horses, but not the horses Alice was used to, trotted over. They were not the colors Alice had expected, and their ears hung down like a Basset Hound's. But perhaps the strangest part was that the saddle already seemed to be built in. A mass on their back had the horn and everything. Perhaps they'd looked like the regular horse she was used to at some point, but evolution had done riders a solid since then.

Tucker let them out into a fenced-in area to trot around and stretch their legs. "That lavender one there," he said, pointing to the periwinkle one, "is named Lucky. She's a good girl. She could carry any two of you on her back and be fine for miles at a time without a rest. I'll send you with Boyd there, too. She's not as strong, but she's focused and takes commands well."

Alice arched a brow at Tucker, but he didn't look her way.

It turned out to be just fine that Boyd wasn't as strong. Vel and Caid doubled up on her, minimizing the weight on her back.

Carefully, Alice reached up and grabbed Lucky's saddle horn. It was solid enough and felt like it was made of bone.

"Yep, right there," said Tucker. "Need a lift up?"

"Nope, I got it." Alice used the horn and threw a leg up and over. The saddle shape appeared to be a thick layer of fat, and it felt both wildly comfortable and disturbingly wiggly as she settled in with it between her thighs. She gave Dan an arm up, and he slipped on behind her.

"That way," said Tucker, pointing to the horizon. "Just straight, and you'll get there. The girls know the way, even if you don't." Alice gave Lucky a gentle heel, and off they went.

But not before she stole one last bewildered look at the man behind them.

CHAPTER
FIFTEEN

"Why were you being so weird back there?" Dan asked, jolting with each step of the horse below him.

"Don't you remember?" said Vel from beside them. "Alice knew someone named Tucker."

"Damn, Susy, you *do* listen to what I say," said Alice. "Yeah, I knew a Tucker King growing up."

"And he looked something like this one?" Dan asked.

"No. He looked *exactly* like this one. Last time I saw him was Christmas break my second junior year of college. Big bonfire. Saw him there. He had a girlfriend from his community college with him, though. But damn if he didn't look just like that. *Just* like that."

"I hear passion in those words," said Caid. "Were you romantic with him?"

"Nah. I mean, not really. Yeah, he was my boyfriend when I was thirteen. My first one. I'd been crushing on him since fifth grade, and he finally noticed me once I grew some hips and tits, I guess. It wasn't a real romance, though. He did kiss me on the Ferris wheel once. We'd both been eating cotton candy, and it was all over our lips. We got stuck together."

"Mmm, I see," said Caid. "And yet romance is romance. I've met many Earthlings, and from what I know, your heart centers develop faster than your minds. They are active from a young, young age. Perhaps you shouldn't discount your relationship with Tucker. I can hear the longing in your words for those times. Was there heartbreak at the end of it?"

Alice thought hard about that. "Not for me. He was a nice boy. Too nice, probably. He liked me a lot, so he wasn't mean to me when I ditched him. I wrote him a letter saying I didn't like him anymore, and that was that."

No one said anything, and Alice felt the judgment in the silence. "I was *thirteen*. I stopped having a crush on him. What was I supposed to do, stick it out until we were sixteen, marry him, and pop out kids together?"

"No one said anything," replied Vel.

"Y'all didn't have to. I could feel what you were thinking."

"Watch out, Caid," said Vel. "Looks like you might not be the only empath in the group."

"Had you forgotten about him until now?" Dan asked.

"Not at all. I've found myself thinking about him a few times since leaving Earth. Random moments, too. And then, *blam*! There's his look-alike. A more complicated person might be asking what it means." Alice pointed ahead. "Town-ho!"

The distant sun was rapidly lowering toward the horizon as the four of them rode into the dusty town. It reminded Alice of something out of the Wild West, with its brown wooden buildings. However, before they entered the town itself, they passed through a parking lot of small spacecraft. Tourists?

"I'll admit," said Dan as they rode the horses at a slow pace between the first few buildings of the main avenue, "I'm not even sure where to start asking for help."

Alice looked around. "How about there?" She pointed to a building a block down, with a sign hanging outside that said, *Sam's Meats, Ethanol & Hats.*

She wasn't sure why that was the place that stood out to her, other than she would really like a hat to keep her head warmer in the cold. And to look awesome.

"As good as anywhere," said Vel, and they rode over and tied up the horses.

Tying up a horse was well within in Alice's skill set, and in general, she felt like she might thrive in a town like this one, should they never be able to get off planet. It wouldn't be the worst of the places they'd visited to spend their remaining days until the drilling erased it all. Maybe she could even pay Tucker a few visits...

But when they stepped inside Sam's Meats, Ethanol & Hats, all thoughts of Tucker were booted right out of her mind.

Sure, the booze along the walls was alluring, and yeah, the brimmed hats on display looked super badass and she wanted one, but what her attention fell to and then fixated on was the man behind the counter who greeted them as they entered. "Howdy, strangers!"

Alice felt like pulling a Dan and slapping herself in the face.

While Vel and Caid strolled further into the store to speak with the clerk, Dan paused, sensing fear nearby, and turned to where Alice had planted herself by the door. "What is it?"

She stiffly waved him closer. "You're not gonna believe this," she said, "but that's Sam Harzheim if I ever saw him."

Dan's eyes grew larger. "Is that someone I should know? Is he dangerous?"

Alice shook her head. "It's weirder than that. He was my homecoming date."

Dan whipped his head around. "*That* guy?"

"That guy."

"But it can't be that guy."

"It is that guy."

"Are you saying he somehow made it off planet?"

"I reckon."

"Hmm... This is certainly improbable."

Vel and Caid were already chatting with the man behind the counter about the nature of their shipwreck when Alice cautiously approached. She wished she'd put a little more time into her hair, maybe swiped on some mascara.

Leaning an elbow on the counter, she smiled and waited for him to notice her.

He gave her a sweeping glance then returned to the conversation. "Nah, he's your guy. I'm telling you, he can fix anything you throw at him. And if he struggles with it, he'll stick with the job until it's done. Good guy."

Alice cleared her throat, and Vel shot her a sideways glance. "You have something to add?"

Alice twirled a piece of hair around her finger. "Nope." She shot the clerk an inviting look.

"I'm Dan," said Dan.

"Sam," said Sam. "And you said you're... Vel? And Caid?"

Caid bowed his head.

"It's a pleasure to meet y'all. If you're not in a hurry, feel free to browse the store, and let me know if you need help with anything. We offer custom hats, but there are a few in standard sizes for purchase."

"I think we're all set on that, but thank you so much for the help," Vel said. She nodded for them to leave, and everyone did but Alice, who stayed at the counter.

Sam blinked at her. "Uh, can I help you, miss?"

"Do you recognize me?"

He pressed his lips together, squinting at her. "I reckon you look a little familiar, but I can't place it. You ever been out this way before?"

"Never."

"Then we don't know each other. I've never been outside of Partner."

"Partner? Is that what this place is called?" It felt good to talk with him again, even if he didn't remember their time together and was inexplicably not the same Sam she knew in high school.

Sam nodded, then his gaze shifted over her shoulder. "I think your friends are waiting on you."

With a sigh, she straightened. "I'm sure they are. Hey, before I go: I'm sorry I split at the homecoming dance. Katie Mae probably would've been fine if I hadn't tracked her down. Herpes isn't always contagious, anyway. You and me were having such a good time, and you were being so nice." She met his eyes and saw only confusion there. "Anyway, sorry I left you at the dance. I wish I hadn't. If I could do it all over again, I'd do something else, like stick around." She patted the countertop and turned to leave.

"What's your name?" he called after her.

"Alice."

"Then apology accepted, Alice."

She caught up with the others by the horses. As Vel untied hers, she said, "What was that about?"

Alice shrugged. "That was my homecoming date."

"A homecoming date?" Caid asked wistfully. "I'm not sure what that is, but it sounds *lovely*."

"It's a dance that high schools do every year toward the end of football season. They invite all the alumni back for the game, and then the students have a dance afterward. Sam went to the bigger high school nearby and asked me to be his date, and I said yes. Nice guy. Star wide receiver. Honor roll. Beautiful eyes, as y'all just weirdly and inexplicably saw for yourself."

"That wasn't him," Vel said. "It couldn't be."

"I reckon you're right, Susy. I reckon you're right. But I can't make heads nor tails of it. He accepted my apology for splitting on him at the homecoming dance."

Dan rubbed at his chin. "I see a pattern here, but I don't like it."

"Same and same," said Alice.

"And I don't understand how it's possible," Dan added.

Alice finished untying Lucky and clapped the Pangolian on the back. "Also same. But I bet not understanding things is scarier for you. I'm used to it by now." She pulled herself onto the horse and offered Dan a hand, and soon the four of them were heading farther into town.

The sun disappeared below the horizon in a dramatic display of neon pink and orange, and it was as if someone had simply turned off the light switch. The night sky exploded with stars above them before a scattering of lamps switched on automatically, lining the dusty road.

Vel took the lead on Boyd, with Caid pretending to sit behind her. She was the only one who'd listened well to Sam's instructions on whom to talk to about the ship part and where to find him. Lucky followed her friend without requiring any direction, freeing up both of her riders, Alice and Dan, to take in the sights of Partner.

"I would do anything to read up on this history of this place," said Dan. "It's pretty obvious that Depot colonization played a big part, given how many Homo sapiens there are, but look at that guy." He pointed to the little being galloping by on six invertebrate legs. "I've never seen that species or even read about it. I have no idea where we are in the multiverse!"

"I don't see any obvious Depot people here now," Alice said. "Maybe they're dressed up in chaps and vests like everyone else."

"Unlikely," said Dan. "The Depot cares too much about its branding to ignore it. And it's not like they have a reason to keep undercover employees on distant planets. The personnel costs would be extraordinary. More than likely, they established this outpost a while back and now simply trade with it. You've seen how in demand things like cowboy boots are in places like Britannica. No doubt the Depot is getting a cut off the tourism here, too. Maybe a fifteen to twenty percent tax..."

Alice nodded along as Dan continued his musings about the Depot's arrangements, but presently, and perhaps for the first time, she was feeling significantly more paranoid about things than he was.

Eight years in College Station didn't teach her much, but she did learn, albeit indirectly, the Universal Law of Exes. This is, of course, the law that states that any two beings who have become quantum and/or emotionally entangled will later run into each other at least once in a space-time location where neither would likely be otherwise.

Just because Tucker and Sam may not *technically* be the same people didn't make much of a difference to her. She agreed with Dan that there was an ugly and unfortunate pattern unfolding in Partner, and while she wished it wouldn't continue, she knew crossing her fingers about it could only do so much. So instead, she kept an eye out for the next one.

She spotted him soon enough.

To their left, wedged between a feed store and a haberdashery, was a small outdoor theater setup. It included a small projection screen and rows and rows of long wooden benches that were filled from end to end by those watching.

Alice didn't recognize the movie being projected onto the screen, but she knew against her will the hallmarks of a hard-boiled detective film.

She pulled on Lucky's reins as her intuition tingled. An ex was near. But who? Surely not *him*…

On screen, an octopus of a being in a fedora sat behind a wooden desk overrun by loose papers and brown folders. Light from outside his office penetrated his lowered window blinds, casting dark stripes of shadow across his invertebrate face. He grabbed a small rodent off his desk and took a bite of it, masticating the thing languidly as he eyed the dame across from him.

"Notice those shadows?" came a man's voice from the crowd, speaking loud enough to be heard over the film's dialogue and saxophone score. "See the way they sit diagonally across his face? The angle of the shadows offsets the canting of the frame, which is designed to make you feel as off balance as he does after this beautiful gal walks into his office and tells him what she knows. The lines created by the blinds give the feeling of metal bars, implying that he's already trapped in a prison of his own making, even if he doesn't know it yet."

Alice scanned the audience for the source of the voice. She'd definitely heard this lecture before. Except it was in a rundown apartment with a *Scarface* poster right above the television. She'd been eating ramen at the time, and she'd found the chicken-flavored ramen vastly more interesting than the lecture.

"I don't know if now's the time to stop and watch a movie," Dan said from behind her.

She shushed him and kept searching for the face she knew she would find eventually.

A man got out of his seat and stood in front of the screen. "See the shadows?" he pointed to them.

Gavin. She knew it.

"And if you'll notice the exquisite *mise-en-scène*…"

"What is it?" Dan asked. He followed her gaze. "Wait, don't tell me…"

"Gavin Anderson." She rocked her head back and groaned. "Why? Why did I waste so much time on him? I can't tell you how many hours I spent pretending to care about cinematic techniques of the fifties and sixties. And for what? So he could fingerbang me dry like he was trying to unclog a drain?"

As the film rolled on, a hand went up in the crowd, and Gavin called on the person.

"Don't you think that, in this case, the femme fatale archetype has slipped into a two-dimensional stock character?"

"Listen," said Gavin, "and understand that I say this as a male feminist, but you can't have your cake and eat it too, Beth. You can't want more women to appear in film and then criticize all the female roles. It's catty, frankly. If you'll stop interrupting the film and actually watch it, you'll see how complex she becomes as the mystery unfolds."

"But making her a plot device doesn't necessarily add—"

"You're clearly not a feminist, *Beth*. Maybe search yourself for internalized misogyny before you try to critique *anything* in Maxim Fortuna's collection. He was a genius. He understood the complexities of females more than most females do."

Another audience member pipped in, "He killed three of his four wives."

Gavin glared at the gentleman who'd spoken. "If you're going to maintain a narrow mind by taking a purely biographical approach, then maybe you should just leave, Gene."

"But Maxim Fortuna *was* one of the most notorious sexual predators in his star system," said another audience member. "And I agree with the lady who said Lindy was a stock character, not an archetype."

Gavin threw his arms into the air. "You know what? Fine." He stomped over to the projector, and a second later the image on the screen disappeared. But the screen only remained blank for a moment. "I'm clearly surrounded by people who have missed out on the basics of capturing life's essence. You think Lindy is a stock character? Please. Take a look at this."

New footage began rolling. It looked to be from a busy square in Partner. Locals walked every which way on their daily routine. Cacophonous music played along with it. The camera zoomed in on one woman, so close you could see her pores. She was staring blankly ahead, possibly waiting for someone or something. "You might think you know women, but have you ever really studied them? Look at the vacancy on her face."

"What in the void?" came a voice from the audience. "That's me. You've been filming me, Gavin?"

He pointed at the women. "Hush, Gale." Jogging to stand in front of the screen again, he opened his arms to the audience. "You're going to tell me *she's* two-dimensional? She's a living, breathing woman! This is what women are like in real life! Lindy holds *ten times* the interest of this subject. I mean, look at her! There's nothing behind those eyes. No mystery, no intrigue."

"Get chapped, Gavin!" Gale stood and scooted past the others on her bench, marching away.

At the front, Gavin shook his head. "Tsk, tsk. Some women really believe they're in competition with one another. Women can be such misogynists, you know. So sad."

Dan leaned slightly forward in the saddle. "Was the one you knew like that, too?"

"Nah," said Alice. "He wasn't so... Actually." She remembered *The Deer Hunter* night at his place. The headband he'd made her wear. The toy six-shooter. Anything for an "immersive experience."

"Yeah, he was. Maybe worse."

"And you stayed with him?"

"I dunno if I was ever with him, really. Sometimes I thought I had him, then he'd disappear for a week, not return my calls, show up at a party with some other girl. Then he'd text me later that night: *U up?* Christ." She rubbed a chilly hand down her face. "I think we had a year of that. I gave up a few times."

"What happened then?"

"He'd call me crying. He'd beg me to come over, say I

was his muse. And my dumb ass would do it. I'd drop everything and hop on over there. One time he called me crying because his cat died. I felt bad for him, but I didn't need to, because I saw the cat a few weeks later. When I called him on it, he told me the lie was out of desperation." She paused, a new thought forming. "Do ya reckon he was just a piece of shit?"

Dan stared at the Gavin beside the projector, who was yelling at the entire audience now. "Even in the most improbable of times, that seems likely."

She shot Gavin the finger, though he was too busy insulting his audience to notice. "We'd better get on getting on." Alice gave Lucky a heel, and the horse was happy to catch up to its friend farther on down the road.

CHAPTER
SIXTEEN

Vel glanced over her shoulder, past Caid. "What kept you two?"

"Another one of her exes," Dan said.

"I don't know what it says about you that your failed romances can populate an entire town," said Vel.

"Not the *whole* town, Susy," Alice said. "There are plenty of people here I haven't— Whoop."

A man strolled by, heading the other direction, and tipped his hat to Alice.

"Another?" Dan asked incredulously.

"It was for, like, *a week* freshman year of college. He sat next to me in communications class and swiped his meal card for me at the dining hall a few times. Then he found out his high school ex was seven months pregnant with his baby, so we stopped talking."

"Still seems like a lot of people," said Vel.

"I've lived a full life. Sue me. And besides, I wouldn't even call some of these dudes exes. More like *run-ins*. Situationships. Take her, for instance." Alice pointed to a petite girl with tan skin and auburn hair who carried a basket of fruit on a crooked elbow. "We made out a few times, tailgated together, and that was that. I started dating Jacob, and it was over with her."

The woman passed by without noticing Alice at all.

"And him," Alice continued, gesturing at a man playing the harmonica on the front step of a saloon, "that's just Esteban. We hooked up once in high school. Hardly an ex."

As Alice continued to point out familiar faces—the physics professor who dealt magic mushrooms, the one with a record of breaking and entering, and so on—Vel was no longer able to hide her smug grin.

"You might want to consider the possibility," Alice said, "that with these improbability waves fucking around like they are, we could just as easily end up on *your* Planet of the Exes, Susy. So maybe stay humble."

"It would be a sparsely populated planet," Vel conceded.

"Mine would be deserted," Dan lamented. "I was young when I left Pangoliarch, and before that, I was so absorbed in my studies that I never bothered with romance."

Nobody asked Caid what his planet would be like; they were all sick of bearing witness to his unabashed romance with Celeste. Best not to invite that conversation.

"You haven't found romance since?" Alice asked. "Nothing in your travels as minister of weapons and culture? Come on, you're practically a knight in shining armor. There have to be ladies—or men—or all the other sexes—out there who are into plated skin."

"If there are, I haven't found them. Romance is off the

table for me anyway. I'm only in one place for a few days at a time, max."

"But that's *perfect*," Alice insisted. "You can hit it and quit it!"

"Not my style," said Dan. "And besides, you don't know what you'll pick up."

"Have *you* been 'hitting it and quitting it' since you started with the Depot?" asked Vel.

Alice frowned. "No. I guess I haven't. Huh." She squinted. "That doesn't sound like me."

They rode on.

"How much farther until we find the place with the parts?" Alice asked.

Vel was keeping track of the landmarks, since that was all Sam had given her to navigate by. The place was such an illogical hodgepodge of old technology and new, and somewhere along the way, no one had thought to add void-blasted street signs.

The sound of Gavin's guerilla film had faded a few blocks back, and as they passed a small alleyway between buildings, a new sound arose.

Grunting. Shouting. Begging.

Having taken the lead, Vel saw the commotion first, and was off her horse without a second thought, sprinting toward the back-alley brawl. "Hey!"

Alice was right on her heels. "Knock that shit off!"

In the darkness of the alley, two men and one woman were absolutely handing some poor fool his ass. Vel grabbed the smaller of the two men first, catching him off guard and yanking him away. He tumbled backward, and she went for the woman next.

Alice took the second man, shoving him off, then

turned to check on the victim, who was curled in a tight ball on the ground, whimpering pathetically. "You okay?"

"No," came the reply. "I didn't do anything. They just attacked me."

It was a man's voice, but weak and tinny from the ass-whooping.

As Dan arrived and Vel ran off the assailants with a flash of the arsenal strapped under her fur coat, Alice reached forward and placed a gentle hand on the man's shoulder. "You good, my guy? Anything broken?"

When he uncurled and looked up at her, a sliver of streetlight spilled over his face.

Alice gasped and took a step back.

Then she took a step forward and aimed the toe of her boot right at his nose.

Vel grabbed her, and Alice's kick caught only air. The man on the ground curled up again.

"What are you doing?" Vel demanded, as Dan rushed in and knelt next to the beaten man.

"Goddamn Matt Growski!" Alice yelled. "I didn't have a blaster then, Matt, but I do now! Threaten me again, motherfucker!"

The man on the ground stared wide-eyed at her, a trickle of blood from his nose curving around his upper lip and dripping into his shirt. "What'd I do?"

"Nothing," said Vel, holding Alice back. "I'm sorry. She's not well. Dan?"

He nodded and continued to tend to the injured victim.

Vel shoved Alice back further, hoping some space might cool her off. "That's not him," Vel said. "Whoever you think it is, it's not actually him."

Dan hollered, "His name *is* Matt Growski, oddly enough. He just told me."

Vel grunted. "Not helping, Dan." Gripping Alice's shoulders, she forced the Texan to look at her. "That's not him."

Alice's jaw was clenched like Vel had never seen it before. She wore the look of an animal in frenzy. Thick puffs of steam spiraled out of her nostrils in the cold air. Alice had gone feral, and it wouldn't have come as a shock to Vel if she'd begun stamping her foot like a pissed-off bull.

"Alice," Vel said more quietly. "We're on a foreign planet in a distant galaxy from yours. It's not him."

That seemed to do the trick, and Alice blinked and inhaled deeply, puffing up her chest. "Yes. You're right. It's not him." She shook her head and laughed dryly. "Oh wow. I had no idea all that was waiting around in me. Hot damn. I'm as shocked as you, Susy." She flapped her hands and rolled her neck. "Okay, I'm good. Of course it's not him. You can let me go."

"Promise?"

"Yep. I got my head on straight."

"I don't think you've ever had your head on straight, but fine." Vel let go of her shoulders, and Alice didn't immediately run after the guy again.

"I think he needs some medical attention," Dan said, helping the man to his feet. "His nose is bloody, possibly broken, and it's painful for him to breathe. Maybe a couple of broken ribs."

"I don't see how that's our problem," Alice said, glaring at the victim.

Vel shot her a scolding look.

"Fiiine. Let's get him to whatever passes as a hospital in this place. A barber, maybe?"

Caid, who had temporarily changed into Gary Cooper but returned to his usual form before anyone who might recognize that saw him, was still waiting with the horses. While he couldn't grab their reins to keep them from walking off, he didn't need to. He had his palms by each of their foreheads and was whispering softly to them. The animals didn't appear to have a care in the world as they kept their heads bowed. "Everything okay?" he asked as the others emerged from the alley.

"I wouldn't say so," Vel replied. "For one, we're still stuck on this planet while the Depot drills away at the edge of the universe. For another, we now have an errand to run."

Caid cast sad eyes on Matt Growski's bloody face. "Poor man."

"Stay with the horses," Alice said. "We'll drop this loser off somewhere as quickly as possible and meet you back here."

Though he appeared to struggle with basic cognitive tasks, Matt was able to lead them to a medic's station two blocks away. Alice banged on the front door while Dan and Vel kept Matt on his feet.

A woman answered, poking her head out, and Alice was instantly relieved that she didn't recognize her. "Special delivery."

The nurse was a petite thing, dressed in a long black smock. She leaned to look past Alice, and her face tightened when she saw who was there. "You gotta be kidding me. Okay, bring him in."

Matt continued to whimper with each step as they

dragged him inside the small space. It reminded Alice of the school nurse's office, with little more than a bed that could be easily sanitized, an uncomfortable chair, and a stocked medicine cabinet. She wondered if all the medicines had expired here, too, or if that was only in Slip'n'Fall.

They dropped him onto the bed, where he remained sitting, and Alice took a post up against the far wall, crossing her arms over her chest to keep her fists from getting away from her.

"Hello, Matt," the nurse said, taking out a small bottle of antiseptic, unscrewing the top, and setting both on the counter next to a glass jar full of cotton balls. "Fancy seeing you here."

His eyes uncrossed just long enough for him to say, "Francine, I'm so glad—"

He didn't get to finish, because Francine slapped the rest of the words right out of him. Though she was small, her aim was sharp, and she nailed him in the cheek in such a way that blood from his nose splattered across Vel's fur coat.

Alice's mouth fell open in a wide grin.

"You piece of horseshit," Francine snapped as Matt whimpered and touched his face where her palm had landed. "I'm not treating a scratch on you until you apologize for what you did to me, and swear you'll turn yourself into a Depot officer for it."

"What'd he do to you?" Dan asked.

Francine didn't answer. She glared at Matt. "Tell them what you did to me."

"Francine, I don't know what you're talking about. If I knew, I'd say it."

"Nuh-uh." She screwed the cap back on the bottle and

shoved it back in the cabinet. "I'm not helping you until you drop that act."

He held up his hands in a preemptive defensive posture. "Listen, if I did something to you—"

"*IF* YOU DID SOMETHING?" She was on her feet now.

"You know I get lost in the bottle sometimes, Francine. I black out. I don't know what—"

She slapped him again, and nobody tried to intervene.

"Get out," she said. "These three ain't your friends, and they're loaded with blasters. Or maybe you're too drunk to realize their coats bulge in strange places. You can either get out right now, or I can tell these folks what you did to me. If they have any decency in them, they won't hesitate to blast your cock right off you."

In solidarity, Alice pulled open one side of her furs and showed Matt what she was working with.

He whimpered as he got to his feet and shuffled toward the door. Pausing before it, he said, "Francine, I wish I knew what you were so mad at me about. I thought we had something."

Francine didn't blink. "I'll hunt you for sport if you ever set foot in here again."

"Gawddamn," Alice muttered.

Once Matt was gone, Francine turned to the others, a perfectly pleasant smile on her face. "Don't worry, you couldn't have known who you were bringing to me. I'm not upset with you."

"I hope not," said Vel. "Mostly because being hunted for sport is the last complication I need in my life right now."

"Out of curiosity," said Alice, pushing off the wall, "what did that dipshit do to you?"

Francine explained as the three strangers listened. Dan's expression morphed to one of shock, Vel's lips curled into a snarl of contempt, and Alice nodded along.

"I believe that," she said. "He did the same thing to me on a distant planet."

"That doesn't make any logical sense," said Francine, "but somehow I still believe it."

CHAPTER
SEVENTEEN

"I wish I'd gotten mad about it," Alice said as they rejoined Caid and mounted their horses again.

"That wasn't you mad back in the alley?" Dan asked.

Alice considered it. "Guess it was. I reckon I've been mad this whole time and just didn't realize it." She paused. "Damn, Susy, I wish you would've let me get just one kick in."

"If I knew then what I know now, I would've. The tinker Sam told me about is just up here."

They turned a corner away from the main street, and the maintained buildings gave way to a small shop surrounded by piles of scrap metal.

"This is it." Vel dismounted and led Boyd over to the hitching post. "Our best bet for getting back off this planet."

"Fingers crossed," said Alice. "I'd rather live on a diet of Hypha than spend my remaining time in Partner. If we can't get outta here, I'll be praying for the Depot to destroy the arrow of time so this whole thing never happened."

"You sound like the Bacc'joons now," said Dan.

Alice cringed. "I don't love that, but I'm certainly understanding their position better, no wife killing required."

Casting a dark shadow on the shop door, Vel knocked and waited to see if anyone was inside. "I have no idea what time it is here or how the hours work. It's possible that the tinker has already closed up shop for the day and gone home."

But that wasn't the case, and the door opened a moment later.

Light from inside presented the person in the doorway as a dark silhouette.

"Hello, strangers. Can I help you?"

Alice froze. "Aw, hell no." She didn't need to see him to know who this was. She recognized the voice. It was the last one she'd heard before taking the job with the Depot.

"No?" he asked.

Vel intervened. "Sorry, she's not well. Ignore her. Our ship crashed on this planet, and we heard you might be the best bet for getting the parts we need to get her up and flying again. Sam sent us."

"Oh! Well, if Sam sent you, then you must be good people. Yes, come on in!" He stepped out of the way and ushered them inside.

The shop was not a shop. It was, in fact, a cozy and spotless house. It was also incredibly warm, and as Alice stepped farther inside, she spotted the fireplace that was the source of the warmth.

"You must be cold," said the tinker. "I'll have Allison bring you some hot tea. Are you hungry? I've been slow-cooking a roast in the oven all day, and it's almost ready. There's plenty to share."

Caid stayed close to Alice, and when he wouldn't be overheard said, "There's a lot of pain associated with this one, isn't there?"

"No. It's just… complicated."

"Matters of the heart usually are."

The tinker led them into the living room, where he invited them to sit down in front of the fire. "Warm up, and we'll have some hot tea for you soon. You look weary. I'll make sure it's caffeinated." He winked, and Alice felt her insides crawl. The same restlessness she experienced after moving in with him was returning in full force.

Dan was more than happy to take a load off by the fire, and he settled into a brown leather armchair. However, as soon as he looked up and caught sight of Alice's expression, he paused. "Oh. He's one of them, isn't he?"

She nodded.

"A good one or a bad one?"

"A good one. A very, very good one. Obnoxiously good."

The tinker returned with a petite blonde woman at his side. She wore an apron and carried a tray with a teapot and four ceramic cups. The tinker must not have realized that one of his guests couldn't technically consume liquids.

"Allison, this is— Oh, goodness! I haven't even asked your names! What a rude host I am!"

"I would argue the opposite," said Caid. "You didn't even know our names and you still invited us in from the cold."

Allison set the tray on a low table in the center of the semicircle of sofa and armchairs. "It's still quite hot. I brought some sweetener in case you want to feel *extra* indulgent. I'm Allison, by the way. It's a pleasure to meet each of you. Jake tells me you're in quite a predicament with your ship." She stared admiringly at the man beside her, and he put an arm around her shoulder.

"I'm Dan Zone, this is Caid Sonorian, Susy Machiavelli, and, uh, Alice Luck."

Jake showed no signs of recognition at the final name in the list, and Alice felt both relief and, frankly, a not inconsiderable amount of resentment about that. She lowered herself into one of the comfortable chairs all the same.

Allison and Jake settled in next to each other on the couch, and the hostess poured the four drinks. She held up a cup at a time, asking each of the guests, "Sweetener?" Each declined. When she made it to Caid, he said, "No, and I hope you'll excuse me for not mentioning it sooner, but…" He waved a hand through the sofa arm. "Holographic. It smells delightful, though."

Alice only just resisted saying, "You can smell?"

Allison offered Caid's mug instead to Jake, who accepted it with a grin and then leaned back, crossing an ankle over his knee. "I'm letting the roast rest for a minute on the stovetop, but you let us know if you need anything else. In the meantime, please, let's get down to business, because I'm sure you've had a long day. What sort of ship are we looking at here?"

As Vel explained the specifications, Alice stared unabashedly at Allison.

Was that what Jacob had wanted her to be? Had he hoped she would wear a goddamn apron around the house and make hot tea for guests? Could Allison really be happy in this sort of environment? Could anyone? It felt like a habitat for housewives, not a home.

Allison's eye twitched, and she hunched her shoulders uncomfortably. Jake interrupted himself midsentence to turn to her. "You okay, babe? What is it?"

She balled her hands into fists and returned to her regularly scheduled pleasant expression. "Nothing, babe. Just a supernova. Nothing close enough to worry about."

He nodded, but didn't look entirely convinced, and pulled the pillow from behind his lower back to slide it in behind her for added support.

Alice wondered if, at that precise moment, Allison was wearing period panties that she had not picked out for herself.

Why am I being bitter about this? I left him.

If Alice had ever been in love, it was with Jacob. He was… nice? Was that enough?

His love felt like a pillow over the face at times, but he'd never pulled the shit that other men had. He'd never lectured and belittled her like Gavin. And he'd certainly never forced himself on her in the way Matt had. This living room, this little wifey, even the roast—it was Jacob's happily ever after.

Had he ever found that back on Earth after she left? Had ditching him and that lame ring in the champagne glass on the rooftop in Austin, Texas, U.S.A., Blerg VFP69, Milky Way, been the best thing that ever happened to him?

All the complicated thoughts made her skin crawl in a familiar way. She wiggled her toes in her boots and tried not to let herself become spring-loaded for a quick exit.

"A busted graviton dampener is an easy enough fix. Are the comm systems out, too?" Jake asked.

"No," said Vel. "Why?"

"Oh, I was wondering why you don't radio the nearest Depot outpost and have one of their nearby patrollers give you a lift."

Dan cleared his throat and took a long sip of tea.

Alice considered keeping her mouth shut, considered letting "Jake" and Allison continue in their blissfully ignorant happily ever after together, but then she remembered what was at stake. If she had to deal with this, Jacob should too.

She let 'er rip. "Depot can suck it. We're not with them anymore."

Allison reached for Jake's hand, and he gripped hers in his lap.

"Oh," he said. "Um. You're not Depot? I assumed with the DeepCUT…"

"Nah," said Alice. "I'll be honest with you. We're with the Alliance. We were trying to get somewhere else, but these dang improbability waves keep coming. You've probably felt them. Yeah, that's because the Depot is drilling at the edge of our universe and it's screwing with the odds. The more they drill, the stronger and more frequent these waves. For instance, one hit us, threw us into an uncharted space fold, and now I'm here, trapped in hell."

"Hell?" said Allison. "I'm not familiar with that place."

"Lucky you."

Jake stared at her, and she knew that look. There was a storm of quiet judgment brewing there. He wouldn't express it, though. No, instead, he was about to say something backhandedly complimentary. She would've bet the multiverse on it.

"If that's all true," he said, "then you are four of the bravest traitors I've met."

Alice rolled her eyes. "It's true, Jake. Why would we lie about it? We're with the Alliance, and you should be, too, if you want this pretty little home and your pretty little wife to keep existing."

He straightened up. "Are you threatening me, Miss Luck?"

"Nah, the Depot is."

He shook his head. "What you're saying is impossible."

"Improbable," Dan corrected him. "And just the right degree of it."

Jake winced. "You mean it?" He leaned forward. "Man to man, is my wife in danger?"

Dan met his eyes. "Yes. Your wife, you, Partner, everything. And I would know. Danger is my middle name."

"I thought it was your first name," said Alice.

"It's both."

"Danger Danger?" she murmured, trying to understand.

Jake set his jaw. "If you say this is the real deal, then I don't have much of a choice. Take me to the ship, and I'll get it up and running if I can."

"But Jakey," said Allison. "What about the roast?"

He stood, staring determinedly ahead. "I'll eat it cold. A man's gotta do what a man's gotta do."

"You could heat it up later," Alice suggested.

"Yeah," said Dan, "just save the juices and drizzle them on top. Should still be moist if you do that."

"There's no time for discussion," Jake declared. "Let's get to your ship right away."

Dan gulped down the rest of his tea, and then the crew followed Jake out of the living room.

The tinker paused at the front door and turned to address his wife. "Don't wait up for me, Allison. Go ahead and eat the roast while it's hot. I'll manage just fine for myself."

"Seriously," said Alice, "you can totally reheat it and it'll be great."

Jake fetched his horse and loaded the tools and parts he'd need into a knapsack that he threw around his shoulder. Then the five of them trotted back through town toward the downed DeepCUT.

Perhaps, if they hurried, everything you've just read would remain imprinted along the arrow of time. Or maybe this page and all the words on it will someday never have existed.

CHAPTER
EIGHTEEN

"It's not as bad as I thought it'd be." Jake was crouched beside an open panel inside the cargo port of the ship, staring at bits and pieces that made Alice's eyes cross. With a hard tug, he yanked out a small metal pipe and held up to the light to inspect. "Yeah, that's it," he said.

Alice couldn't hang around watching anymore. "I'm gonna take the horses back to Tucker."

"Need help?" asked Dan, who appeared nearly as bored as Alice.

"Nah. Thanks, though. Go rest up. It wasn't that long ago that you had the world's biggest jitter fit. I'm sure those boosters are wearing off by now."

She walked down the ramp and untied both horses. She could ride them there, but it wasn't far to the cabin, and she could use a little time to think.

You can probably guess what she thought about. It was way more contemplation than she preferred to engage in, and to dive into it would only bring the mood down even lower than it already was. Suffice to say, she was deep in her feels by the time she reached the cabin and led the horses into the pen.

She could've turned around and left at that point, but all that thinking had her tied in knots.

She knocked on the front door instead.

Fifteen wild and ill-advised minutes later, as she was reattaching one of her thigh holsters, she looked over at Tucker where he sat on a blanket by the fire, and said, "You gotta go back to town. Living out here like a hermit? This can't be it. The multiverse could end tomorrow. You really want this to be all you have in the meantime?"

"I can't."

"Ya really can. Look. I can read it all over your face. Someone hurt you. She was probably trying to help her friend, but in the process she broke your heart. Am I close?"

He stared at her wide-eyed but nodded.

"Yeah, that shit happens. And guess what, I'm about you leave you again."

"You could stay."

"I could, but I won't. Now listen. Ya gotta get over it. I know I—*that girl* hurt you, but the answer isn't this weird cabin-core lifestyle, eating that shitty meat. Go into town. Find yourself a girl. There's a nice nurse named Francine who seems pretty badass, and if you treat her right, I reckon she won't hit you."

"That's who broke my heart."

"Oh. Well, there are probably other good women there. And men, if you're a real masochist. Maybe some other sexes. Haven't really looked into how all that works here, so I'm making a lot of assumptions." She pulled on her boots. "My point is that you'll regret leaving it all behind.

The multiverse is a lonely place, and relativity is a fickle bitch. Time slips away fast, and before you know it, all these things you thought didn't matter that much are gone, and it turns out they matter a whole, awful lot. But it's too late to do anything about it by the time you realize that." She slipped on her fur coat, bouncing her shoulders until it felt right. "Don't be a fool like me, Tucker. Don't run away."

"Isn't that exactly what you're doing right now?"

"It was a great fifteen minutes, sure. But we're talking about *you*, my guy. Not me."

"You're literally getting ready to abandon this place forever while you're telling me not to run away—"

"Shh…" She squatted beside him and pressed a finger to his lips. "Less thinking. Trust me. I did a bunch of it on the walk over here, and it got me nowhere." She removed her finger. "Promise me, Tucker. Go give your life a shot in town. No more of this rat meat."

"I'll consider it."

"Do more than that." She leaned in and planted one final kiss on him. "I shouldn't have broken up with you in a letter. I'm sorry."

"What are you talking about?"

She pulled open the door and let the cold night air hit her. "You know," she said, wagging a finger at him. "Deep down, you fucking know."

***

The lights from the ship were easily visible from the doorstep of Tucker's cabin.

A scraggly old tree, all shadows and insinuations, jutted up from the rocky ground to her left like a hand breaking free from a grave.

She tried to shake the image from her mind, remembering the time Gavin had made her watch a movie with that in it and kept pausing every few seconds to explain its cultural significance.

I gotta get off this cursed planet. This place couldn't be the end for her. There had to be more.

She turned her attention to the rocky ground, careful not to roll an ankle in the darkness. To her right, the sun threatened to rise. She was pretty sure it was not the same sun that had set only a couple of hours ago, though she wouldn't have put money on that. For now, there was only a dull haze, like a radioactive glow seeping over the horizon. She kicked a rock, sending it scuttering ahead until it disappeared in the shadows.

She kicked another, and the sound of the porous object knocking into the others was quite satisfying. She kicked hard at a small pile of rocks to increase the effect, and because they went scattering in so many places, creating a clatter, she didn't even notice the other sound of rocks under boots that was growing louder and heading directly at her.

Her body registered the threat a millisecond before her brain did, and she whipped her head to the left just as Matt Growski plowed into her on her blind side.

It was not the kind of terrain one would want to be tackled on, and she felt the air leave her lungs as a large, jagged rock hit her right below the shoulder blade.

The dawn haze illuminated the dried blood on his face as he pinned her arms to the ground, snarling. "I don't know who you are, but if you thought you could kick me when I was down—"

She spat in his face, throwing him off balance enough to free her leg, which she used to knee him in the groin.

He hollered, and she rolled him. "You dumb bitch," she spat. "You think I ain't wrestled bigger hogs than you?" She jerked her hand free of his grip and slipped a blaster from her thigh holster. Then she pressed that to where he clutched his balls. "I'll shoot that schlong right off you. Don't think I won't." She got to her feet, her back and head stinging to high heaven.

"Don't shoot me. Please don't shoot me."

"I ain't some little high school girl anymore, Matt. I've survived assassination attempts, psychotic Splatterpoots, and a heard of hankerchucks. Hell, I've been to Star Cluster B and lived to tell the tale. I ain't scared of you now."

Blood was running fresh from his nose. "Please," he said, holding up a hand. "Please don't shoot me. I'm sorry. I don't know… Sometimes I lose control. Something takes over. It's not me. I don't even know why I did that to you. I don't even know you! Please don't shoot me."

Alice considered it. "I reckon you *don't* know me. But I know you. Francine knows you, too." Her consideration came to a swift conclusion, and she fired. The shot went straight through his thigh, the heat of it destroying and cauterizing flesh at once.

Matt screamed and then continued screaming. "You bitch! You shot me! You stupid bitch! You'll pay!"

"You know I can just shoot you again real easy, right? Maybe you ought to shut your mouth, my guy."

"Do it! Shoot me!"

She aimed the blaster at his head, imagined his brains splattering the porous rocks…

"Nah." She let it fall to her side. "In the words of a guy I once knew, it's only fun if they don't want it."

She put her back to him and walked toward the ship.

Then, when it really settled in that she'd just shot a guy, she checked over her shoulder (he was still whimpering on the ground) and started jogging.

Vel met her halfway back to the ship. She, too, was jogging.

"There you are." Vel gave her a quick scan, and her gaze paused briefly on the spatter of blood on the bottom of Alice's coat. "You okay? We heard screaming."

"Yep, I'm good." Alice looked over her shoulder. She couldn't see the figure of Matt in the distance now. Was he too far away, or had he already limped off? Or maybe Tucker had helped him.

The thought was among the most disconcerting she'd had that day. Nobody liked imagining their exes hanging out.

"You sure? There was a lot of yelling, and you have blood on you."

"Aaaall good."

"There's blood on your coat."

Alice shrugged. "Not mine."

Vel squinted at her and appeared ready to ask more questions, but instead, she nodded. "What happens between you and your exes can stay that way."

They jogged back to the ship, and Alice was grateful to be on familiar territory as they entered the cargo dock. Jake was still working away and Caid was nowhere to be seen as the glass elevator lowered, and Dan hurried off it. "You okay?"

"I'm fine," she said.

He sniffed the air. "Wait, why does it smell like se—"

"Okay, *fine!*" Alice threw her hands in the air. "I shot Matt Growski in the thigh. He might lose the leg. Big whoop."

"That's not what I was going to say," said Dan, "but I'm honestly glad to hear it."

"Same. But I reckon we should get a move on. He seemed very upset about it."

"Why didn't you shoot to kill?" Vel asked. "I would've."

Alice held up a hand. "I don't think Monday-morning quarterbacking is what we need right now, Susy." She approached Jake to check on the progress, but found the man sitting and staring, not touching a thing. "What's the problem?"

"I… I don't think I should help you. I think you're the bad guys."

Alice laughed. "Oh, no, no, no. We're not revisiting this. Listen, Jake." She crouched beside him, but he refused to look at her. "We're not the good guys or the bad guys. We're just guys. Guys trying to keep other guys from erasing all the guys, okay?"

"I don't know," he said. "I've met some very nice folks working for the Depot."

"Yep, *they'll* disappear, too."

"I've always believed the Alliance was bent on destruction. Now you're shooting my friends."

"Fack. Matt Growski is your *friend*?"

"One of my oldest."

"Then I'm sorry to tell you he's a shitbag."

Jake shook his head miserably. "He's always seemed like a good guy to me."

Vel gripped Alice's shoulder. "Don't shoot him. We need him."

Alice rolled her eyes. "Of course I'm not gonna shoot Jake. He's an idiot, but that doesn't warrant a death sentence. Jake, look at me."

He shot her a sideways glance, which would have to do.

"What's really going on here?" she asked.

This was an approach that he'd used on her countless times when she'd done her best to sabotage the relationship. It'd always worked (until it didn't). Turnabout was fair play.

Jake deflated. "What you described with the Depot. The drilling. It's bad. I know it's bad. But I also know that if I help you get off the ground, you'll leave to do whatever it is you plan on doing, and I'll be stuck here with the knowledge of what's going on but no part to play." He met her eyes finally. "Take me with you, Alice. Let me help with whatever this is. I can't stay here wondering if every moment will be my last. I can't just sit here."

Alice placed a hand on his knee. "Here's how it's gonna be, Jake. You're going to stay here. My friends and I are going to fuck off from this Podunk planet and see what we can do. In the meantime, you take care of things here. You weren't made for space. You were made for Allison."

"She's so *compliant!*" He smashed his fist on the wall beside the open panel. "She's so *domestic!*" His face was red, and he stared straight ahead. "I can't take it anymore!"

"Yes, you can. And you will. You may not believe me, but this is a time-tested formula. You stay here, I leave. It's what I do. Maybe I shouldn't, but if I hadn't, I wouldn't be here. We never would've found out about the drilling, and we never would've known to stop it. And now I've found a problem that I can't run away from, and so I have no choice but to face it." She smiled, staring into his confused eyes. "So maybe there *is* a reason for it all. Maybe all my running was part of a bigger plan. Or...

maybe it wasn't. Maybe it was totally random and all for nothing in the end. But just like I had no choice but to run until I couldn't run anymore, you have no choice but to fix our ship and then go home to Allison."

"I do have a choice," he said.

She booped his nose. "No, ya don't. Because if you don't fix our ship and then fuck off back home to your wife"—Alice got to her feet and drew her blaster—"I'll shoot you in the head."

"Whoa," said Vel.

"Have you lost your mind?" asked Dan.

"Yes," Alice replied. "Now fix the spaceship, Jacob."

As Allura fired up the ship's liftoff systems, Alice, Vel, and Dan stood just inside the port of the loading dock as the ramp slowly rose. With the dusty dawn haze like a sheer curtain between them, Jake had his feet planted on the ruddy ground just outside the ship, staring at the crew for the last time.

"Thanks," said Dan. "Uh, sorry about the threats."

Alice waved *au revoir*. "No hard feelings, Jake. It is what it is."

And just before the port closed completely, she could have sworn she heard him mutter, "Typical."

CHAPTER
NINETEEN

Finally back on the other side of the uncharted space fold, Alice kicked off her boots and put her feet up on the control panel in front of her, crossing her ankles and clasping her hands behind her head. "That was something else, huh?"

"We're not out of the woods yet," said Vel.

"Not even close," added Dan. "With all the time we wasted, we might be *farther* in the woods than we've ever been."

"I love that," said Caid, who it turned out had spent the last hour meditating in his room, which everyone was pretty sure meant quantum vibrational sex with Celeste. "The image of entering the woods is present in many cultures' collective unconscious as a process of confronting danger and darkness, often in the form of our shadow selves."

"I did that once," Alice said. "Too much jungle juice at a frat party. Caught sight of my shadow on the wall and thought it was about to throw a punch. I beat it to it. Or, well, I guess we tied."

"That's not quite what I meant," said Caid, "but it's an enlightening story, nonetheless. Thank you for sharing it."

"Allura."

"Yes, Big Susy?"

"How much time passed at the Alliance HQ while we were on the other side of that space fold?"

"Thirty-one minutes and eleven seconds."

Vel and Dan shared a look. "No, I mean the whole time we were there. We were there for hours, plus the time distortion of a space fold. How much was all of that?"

"You want me to give it to you again, Big Susy? However you like it. It was thirty-one minutes and eleven seconds."

"No, but that can't…" Vel screwed up her face, glaring at the control panel in front of her. "That would mean that the space fold was… inverted?" She looked at Dan. "Is that even possible?"

He appeared as anxious about it as she was. "It's possible. I don't understand how, but time shrinkage, as opposed to dilation, is theoretically possible. More likely, though, is that the Alliance HQ went through a time slip, which changed the relativity from that direction."

"So how much time passed?" Alice asked. "Like, how much closer to the Depot possibly drilling through to the wrong universe are we?"

"It's relative," said Dan and Vel.

"I don't love that," said Alice. "But either way, we'd better hurry up. Feels like we have a ticking clock, even if the clock can't get its shit together on what time it is."

"We're only a quarter of an hour, ship time, away from Putterpantsia. We'll be landing before you know it," said Allura.

As the planet came into view, Alice couldn't help but

notice that it looked like many planets. Perhaps it was selection bias, since they had no reason to visit planets that lacked the ability to preserve life, but the green-and-blue thing was clearly a trend. Sure, plenty of places also offered a variety of colors in their plant life, and not all oceans were nice and blue, but from above, those two colors tended to stand out.

There were, however, large swaths of Putterpantsia where tan and brown were the predominant colors, but that wasn't where the crew landed. Where they landed was green, but also red and orange and a whole palette of other colors that turned out to be rooftops.

Crumbling rooftops?

"Why do we keep landing on planets in disrepair?" Alice asked.

"Mathematically speaking," said Dan, "civilizations spend more time in disrepair or as ruins than they do thriving."

"Who would've thought the artist colony wasn't being properly maintained?" Vel remarked.

Allura landed them on the planet with a sexy jolt.

Putterpantsia hadn't always been full of artists. But two generations earlier, a skirmish broke out within the solar system, one which required every able-bodied adult to join the fight. This left the children quite sad and lonely.

And while many of the adults returned from the war, they were never fully present. They dismissed their children's opinions as unimportant in the face of such atrocity as they had witnessed. Even the wives were vacant and inattentive. Supernovas went totally unmentioned in nearby parts of the galaxy. The children were left to raise themselves, to understand the world around them and find meaning in their deeply ingrained self-loathing. And so it was that Putterpantsia became a hotbed for artistic impulses.

They disembarked on the edge of a bustling village. While the structural integrity of the shops wasn't anything to write home about (assuming one still had a home), the vibrant aesthetics of the place were undeniable.

Alice couldn't help but grin as she took in the fever dream of color. She'd never experienced this vivid of a place outside of that one music festival where she'd taken a pill that she thought was ibuprofen but was definitely not.

The dazzling colors were almost enough to keep her from noticing all the large cockroaches scuttling around.

"Wait, we've met one of these before!" she said, watching a chattering crowd of them wander by. "At the Alliance meeting! Gus! He was cool!"

"I was reading up on Putterpantsia," said Dan, "and the Click'sps—that's what Gus was—are actually the natives of this place. But as you can tell, it's also a popular tourist destination. Plenty of other types of beings."

He was right. The place was almost as diverse as the market on Vongarian, where the Alliance assembly took place.

Vel leaned toward Alice. "Look over there. See the jumpsuits? Strong Depot presence on this planet, so we do need to keep it down about the Alliance while we're here."

Alice narrowed her eyes at Vel then Dan. "Wait, I feel like I missed a brief. How do y'all know so much?"

"You did miss a brief," Vel replied. "We didn't bother sending it to you because we figured you wouldn't read it anyway. But we brushed up before arriving."

"Hold on, is *that* what y'all were reading on the way over?"

"Yes," said Vel. "What did you think we were reading?"

"Dunno. Comics? Alien romance? No judgment from me, of course. Caid, did you know about the brief?"

The hologram was so absorbed in his surroundings that he was neglecting to make the bottoms of his feet line up with the ground. He floated an inch above it as he pantomimed his stroll. "I don't like to bother with briefs. I prefer to remain present and grounded to simply be with those around me. Preconceived notions can create barriers for deep connection." He pressed his hands to his heart. "Look at this place. Really look at it. So much inspiration. So much beauty. All these hearts crying out to be heard, to hear themselves!"

"At least I'm not the only one who didn't read the brief," Alice muttered.

Dan led them toward the heart of the village, which was built on a steep incline. They hiked uphill, catching snippets of conversation as they went:

"Not nearly up to the standard one would expect from a graduate of Bulshun College..."

"I would be too embarrassed to show my portraits to the clients if they looked like that..."

"I found the humor sophomoric at best..."

The crew wound their way along the cracked flagstone streets to a stream that twisted down the side of the hill.

The banks along it had been turned into a peaceful walkway, if one ignored all the crumbling rocks that scattered down the eroding bank, creating a major hazard every few yards. A rickety fence ran between the walkway and the edge of the bank, more as an homage to fences than as any true guard from tumbling into the water.

Along the walkway sat artists by blank canvases. Their attention wasn't focused on the lovely bubbles of the water's surface, but rather eating and chatting with others, even smoking rollies with their weird little cockroach legs.

One artist finished its meal, picked up a brush, dipped it in a rich, ochre-colored paint, and let it hover above the canvas. And then the artist dunked the brush into a cup of water and abandoned whatever thought of beginning had seemed to flare up. Instead, it turned toward the walkway, spotted a familiar face, and yelled, "How's the novel coming?"

A cockroach on the crew's other side replied, "Just had a great idea for an opening line today! Trying to find the time to sit down and put it to page before I forget like I did last time!"

The painter hollered, "Good luck!" then muttered, "You'll need it, you hack."

Closer to the center of town, Dan said, "This looks like a good spot," and led them into what appeared to be a bar. All were relieved that the being tending it was not one of the cockroaches.

"Are we drinking?" Alice asked.

"Wouldn't recommend it," said Dan. "But we should order something. The culture of Putterpantsia is organized around its vices, alcohol being one of them. Because of that, those who serve the alcohol function much the way many cultures' religious leaders do, in that they listen to confessions. However, they aren't bound to secrecy."

"Then why do people divulge?" Vel asked.

Dan shrugged. "They're drunk."

The crew found four seats at the bar in the center of the dark space, and Alice leaned over to Caid, muttering, "You know how you always get people to tell you their secrets? Now would be a good time to turn that up to eleven."

Caid tilted his head to the side. "I sense that you want me to then relay any secrets to you."

"Of course."

"Hmm," said Caid. "That sounds like a breach of trust."

"If they trust a guy they just met with a big, dark secret," said Alice, "that's on them."

"My heart doesn't agree with that," Caid replied.

"Does your brain? Does your brain like the idea of the multiverse not disappearing? End to a means, my guy."

Visibly conflicted, Caid nodded and walked over to a table of cockroaches. She heard him say, "Excuse me, I couldn't help but overhear a snippet of your conversation, and I found it fascinating. I'm new here—would you mind if I joined you to soak in the brilliance?"

"Alice," Dan said. "Drink order."

The bartender was staring at her impatiently through two powder-pink eyes.

"Whatever he ordered is great," she replied, nodding Dan's way.

The bartender was covered in thick maroon fur that disappeared beneath pants held up by suspenders. Like many of the species Alice had encountered, he had two primary arms, and then farther down the body, two auxiliary arms. All four were busy mixing up drinks, as his knobby, fluffball ears twitched atop his large oval head.

As Vel sat up straight, subtly scanning their surroundings for any threats, Dan leaned his elbows on the bar and spoke above the hum of conversation. "You been working here long?"

"About ten years," replied the bartender in a deep, gruff voice.

It was an irrelevant bit of information, since years varied so much from planet to planet. But it was a place to start.

"You do this full-time?"

The bartender shook a drink then poured it into a small glass beaker, where it immediately began to simmer. "Nah. I do it to pay the bills while I pursue my true passion."

"And that is?"

"I'm a writer. Been working on my debut novel for eight years. I think it's almost ready."

"Wow," said Alice, "that must be a thick book!"

"Might be." He added a squirt of something opaque to the simmering liquid. "Not sure yet. I probably won't finish up the first chapter for another few months."

"Oh," said Alice.

"What's it about?" asked Dan.

Nobody really cared, but it kept the bartender interested in himself enough to not wonder why he was being chatted up by these strangers.

The truth was that he never got to talk about his novel. He wanted to, but everyone who pulled up to his bar was too busy talking about *their* novel, or their painting or sculpture or poem or dance routine. Nobody ever asked him about what he was working on.

"It's a meta inspection of the lies we tell to protect ourselves from feelings of intense dismay."

Alice felt her eyelids drifting closed and forced herself to blink away the sudden onset of lethargy.

"Sounds interesting," Dan lied.

"Oh, it is. Thematically, it's in the same vein as Glorpertin's *Inspections* and Fsirng's *Night Sleeps*, but without the emotional redundancy and pedantic tone. Plus, mine has more tits. Or it will, once it's done. I just have to figure out how to add in all the tits, but I'm not worried about that. I have my appointment with the muse next month. The novel will practically write itself after that."

Dan chuckled. "Very nice of the muse to show up at a scheduled time."

But the bartender didn't laugh. Instead, he paused midway through pouring the bubbling concoction into a large copper cup and said, "The muse doesn't show up. You go visit the muse."

"Right, right," said Dan. "Apologies. I'm not an artist like yourself, so I don't know how these things work."

The bartender passed Dan the first completed drink and said, "You know all that stuff I said about Glorpertin and Fsirng? I know what I'm talking about. I'm a well-respected book critic. You might've heard of me. Name's Turb."

"Oh, nice," Dan said, noncommittally, because of course he'd never heard of Turb. "You critique books?"

"I do. I wrote one of the most famous criticisms around. Everyone was fussing about this book that made its way around the solar system. A novel about a young Bindla and his pet fratch. It was being touted as the best novel of the century. I found it redundant and pedantic. So

I wrote a review that said, 'Sophomoric. A perfectly good story ruined by the author's politics. Not at all what I'd hoped it would be.' That was the end of that book! The author's career never recovered. Shame on them for even trying to publish that emotional propaganda, frankly. Shame!" Turb grinned.

"Wow," said Vel flatly, "you're so… powerful."

As Turb puffed up proudly and finished the rest of their drinks, Alice looked around. Caid was deep in conversation at his new table. Good. Maybe *someone* could gather useful information while they were here.

She decided to take a more direct approach with Turb. "You ever heard of a thing called the touchstone?"

Vel put the drinks on the Alliance's secret credit line when Turb slid her a tablet.

"Touchstone? Is that, like, a novel? Oh void, it's not a serialization, is it?" He rolled his rosy eyes. "I can't *stand* those. Written by people who won't shut up. Like, get on with it already. It's so clear serialists never know where they're going. It shows the lack of intelligence in the general population that anyone reads serials."

Alice realized her mouth had fallen open slightly as she tried to follow along with his unprompted rant. "No, it's not a novel. Or a serialization. At least, we don't think it is."

"Then what is it? Oh, *please* tell me it's not a novella or a short story collection." Turb was really enjoying his words now, drawing each of them out and swaying like he might faint if she told him the wrong thing.

"I don't think it's… words. Maybe it is, but that was not my impression until I mentioned it to you. Now you got me wondering, though."

Turb sighed and was clearly losing interest in his new

customers. "Whatever it is, it sounds droll, like it wants to sound edgy and mysterious, but it's merely iterative."

"Sure." Alice checked with Vel to make sure the drinks were paid for, and then she nodded for them to head outside again. They signaled for Caid to come with, and he began wrapping up his conversation at the table.

They found four chairs easily enough at a long table in the sunshine, and for a moment, Alice felt like she was back on Earth, relaxing at a campus bar on the weekend.

Then a bunch of cockroaches walked by, and she returned to reality.

Dan stared down at his drink, assessing it, then appeared to decide against the temptation. "This is going to be trickier than we thought. We know the touchstone is somewhere around here because of the coordinates, but we don't know who might know about it."

"Or who's willing to talk about it rather than themselves," Vel added.

Just then, a being approached. It was slightly shorter than the tabletop and reminded Alice of the Pink Panther Popsicles from the ice cream truck... after the Texas sun had its way with them for a few minutes.

The skin beneath the being's eyes sagged like a hound dog's, giving the creature a morose appearance. It helped itself to the seat reserved for Caid and only then looked around at those sitting near it. "Nice jumpsuits." It rolled its droopy eyes.

"That seat's reserved," Vel said.

"I didn't see a sign." It plunked a full metal mug on the table. "What, you got another jumpsuit waiting to take a load off? Come on, have some pride. A little fashion sense never hurt anyone."

Vel grimaced at the thing. It was wearing what

appeared to be two large nutshells. Each was halved and secured around the being's slender torso with leather straps, one nut on the bottom half, one on the top. Both were splattered with blue and green paint. Vel decided against vocalizing the reply at the tip of her tongue, but only just.

"What kind of artists are you?" the little thing asked.

"We're not artists," replied Dan.

"Tourists." It nodded at its own observation. "Gawkers. I'm an artist. A sculptor." It gulped down its drink.

"What, um, what sort of things do you sculpt?" Dan asked.

When it had finished the contents of its cup, it said, "Not sure yet. Still exploring my voice. My appointment with the muse isn't for another year and a half. I'll have a better idea of what I sculpt then, of course. I'll be off! On a trajectory straight for the stars!"

"A year and a half?" asked Alice. "That's a long time to wait. Why not start today?"

The being squinted at her scornfully. "You're out of your brain. Right out of your brain. How am I supposed to sculpt *before* I see the muse, huh? What am I supposed to do, create boring and uninspired art? You want me to humiliate myself like that? Do you have *any* idea what the critics would say if I started creating before seeing the muse? Do you even know how many critics there are around here?" It glanced around anxiously. "They could be anywhere. For all I know, you three could be critics!"

"Can't everyone be a critic at one time or another?" Dan asked.

The little being looked like it was about to take off

running at the idea, so Alice quickly changed the subject. "Do you know about the touchstone?"

The little thing appeared to consider it. "Yes. I did once think about making a sculpture of someone touching a stone. It wasn't the most inspired idea, of course, but I haven't seen the muse yet, so what can you expect?"

Caid emerged into the sunlight, and Vel told the being to scram, which it did, grumbling about being misunderstood.

"I didn't mean to interrupt," said Caid, taking the seat.

"Get anything good inside?" Alice asked. "Because we didn't. Not inside, not outside."

"Oh yes," said Caid with a grin. "So much good conversation with those fellows. We talked about their mothers almost the entire time!"

"Of course you did," said Vel.

"I meant anything about the touchstone," said Alice. "Anything useful."

Caid bobbed his head. "I feel like it all had *emotional* relevance."

"Not for me," said Vel.

"They never mentioned the touchstone," Caid replied, "though, to be fair, I didn't ask about it. I hoped they would offer it up once they felt safe enough with me."

"That is not how interrogations work," Vel said.

"They did talk effusively about the muse, though."

Alice waved that off. "I think I've heard enough about that."

Caid stroked his chin. "You've heard about it?"

Alice nodded.

"It does feel like an avoidance tactic," Caid conceded. "Claiming that one cannot create art until visiting the muse? If that were the case, hardly any art would ever be made. However, visiting the muse did seem to have an effect on one of the gentlemen I was speaking with."

"He's done it?" Dan said. "I figured no one really had. I thought it was just a figure of speech."

"That was my assumption as well." Caid shrugged. "But he claims he had his appointment already, and I have no reason not to believe him. He's been writing sonnets about the muse ever since. He spoke of the muse as if it were a real thing. He described it as a woman, but not just any woman. A perfect and ageless woman. I began to wonder if—"

"Finally, some jumpsuits!" The raspy voice pulled their attention to a woman in a neon-yellow jumpsuit. She motioned to the tall chair next to Alice. "Anyone sitting here?"

Alice spotted the Depot patch on the arm immediately, but said, "All yours."

The reason Alice didn't protest was that she was too distracted by a single fact: the woman was a Bacc'nali.

Dan and Vel shared a quick look.

The Bacc'nali looked each of them over. "You're not Depot."

"Nope."

"Then what's with the jumpsuits?"

"We find them comfortable."

The woman laughed. "More comfortable than the junk these weirdos are wearing, that's for sure. You're not artists, are you?"

Alice shook her head and offered a reassuring smile.

"Thanks be to HHHH."

Had she just yawned? It sure seemed like it.

"Name's Phoebe. Phoebe Rummager." She held out a hand, and Alice shook it. Phoebe offered a wave to the rest, who were out of arm's reach. "And between you and me, you should be glad you're not Depot. This planet is such a mess. I'm starting to think I was assigned this position because someone up top hates my guts."

"You work here?" Dan asked.

"I try. Supposed to be laying the groundwork for a thriving art marketplace."

"And that's not going well?" asked Alice.

"Are you kidding? Look at this place. Have you seen *any* art to sell? I feel like I'm losing my mind. Everyone's waiting for the muse, then when they get out of their meeting with the muse, *if* they start producing, they're turning out absolute junk! You can't sell someone's first attempt at art. Believe me, I've tried." She drank from a large tankard, then slammed it back on the table.

"You been here long?" Alice asked.

"Too long. Years, whatever that means to you. Two thousand, one hundred and nine days." She shook her head. "I'm starting to think I should've stayed on planet where I belonged and let the Bacc'joons have their way with me like they did everyone else."

"So you *are* Bacc'nali," said Dan.

"Sure am. I wasn't made for this tedious work, I'll tell you that."

"You came here to escape the slaughter?" Dan asked.

"Sure did. That's why any Bacc'nali you're likely to meet now works for the Depot. When things started heating up on Bacc'nalia, the Depot dropped in and offered an escape for some of us. Not everyone, obviously, which was a shame. If I'd known what I'd be spending my life doing, though..." She shook her head.

"And by that, you mean setting up a marketplace?" Dan asked.

"You say that like it's a tiny task. But look at this place. Before the Depot engineers came by, tragic death was through the roof. Buildings and bridges were collapsing left and right because there was no structural integrity. You wouldn't believe the educational campaign we had to run just to convince the locals that dying tragically was *not* ideal. Only once they allowed us to reinforce some of the structures did the death rate drop to something sustainable." She leaned forward, lowering her voice. "Increasing safety was the Depot's worst idea, because why would anyone want *more* people wandering around with too much life to spend doing nothing important?"

Dan noticed that Phoebe was to the end of her drink and slid his toward her. "I haven't touched it."

She stared down at it for a moment before gripping it and saying, "Eh, if it's poisoned, it's poisoned." She took a sip. "So why are you four here? Vacationing?"

Alice understood that she should tread carefully here, since Phoebe worked for the very organization they were trying to take down.

It was unfortunate that treading lightly was not in Alice's skill set. "We're looking for something called the touchstone."

Phoebe's body went rigid, and she looked from face to face, then down to her drink. "Why are you looking for the touchstone?"

"You know about it?"

"Of course I do. But I want to know how you do."

"You say first," said Alice.

"No, you say first."

An impasse. Figured. She knew she was being too direct, even as she'd asked the question. "Forget I even mentioned it," said Alice. "Listen, you wanna see some toes?"

Phoebe perked up. "Toes?"

"Yeah. I have some. Ten of 'em."

"Ten?!" The Bacc'nali's eyes bulged.

"Susy?"

"Yep," said Vel, already getting out of her chair, "I'll go get everyone another round of drinks."

CHAPTER
TWENTY

Twenty minutes later, Alice still had her boots off, and was wiggling her toes to Phoebe's delight.

"I remember hearing about these things growing up, but I never thought I'd actually see them!"

Alice gave a thumbs-up with her big toe, and then she dropped both feet beneath the tabletop and back into her boots.

Phoebe wiped a tear from her eyes. "You live long enough, and you see things you can't even imagine. Hey, you should show those around to some of the locals! Think of the poetry you'd inspire!"

The Bacc'nali was fully drunk, thanks to the tag-team efforts of Vel and Dan, who made sure the drinks kept on coming. It was clear from his somber expression that Caid didn't approve of the plan, which violated basic tenets of consent, but he managed to keep his mouth shut about it.

Alice went fishing. "What about the touchstone? You think I could pick it up with my toes?"

Phoebe guffawed. "I'd like to see you try! No, she's way too big to lift with your toes."

"She?" said Alice, trying not to seem too invested.

"Yeah, the muse."

"No, I said the touchstone."

Phoebe waved it off. "One and the same. Here they call her the muse, but the Depot calls her the touchstone."

"Why two names?"

"She's the touchstone, period. Touchstones are Depot plants. The Depot drops down one of its own for various reasons. Maybe it's to stoke rebellion, maybe it's to introduce a virus, whatever. They have their reasons, don't they?"

"And the touchstone here?" Alice asked. "What's she for?"

"The marketplace, of course! The Depot saw the opportunity of all these artists but couldn't get them to produce. Too many critics. From what I heard, the Depot considered taking out all the critics so the artists could thrive, but then they realized that the critics *were* the artists, so they nixed that. Instead, they sent down the touchstone to get things moving. We found out quickly enough that she needed a rebrand. Everyone here was already waiting for the muse to visit, so those of us working here said, 'Hey, what if we tell everyone that's not how it works, that she doesn't do house calls, but you can get on her schedule?' It was an easy step from waiting for the muse to visit to visiting the muse, so we went around signing everyone up for a time slot. We met some resistance, sure. They thought that being proactive and seeking the muse wouldn't produce real art. There are still a few holdouts, frankly. But we don't care. The muse will never visit them. They'll be waiting forever. They would've met the same fate if the Depot had never come here. Can't help everyone, right?"

"Sounds like it's working, at least," said Alice. "Caid says he had a conversation with someone who had their visit and has been writing sonnets ever since."

Phoebe slumped. "I'd bet my right arm those sonnets are about the muse."

Caid's brows rose. "Yes. That's what he said."

"Figures. That's the problem. When they get their time with the muse, she encourages them to reflect on their life, to extract meaning and beauty that they can then express through their art. I've listened in on her sessions. She's good. One might even say manipulative. The artists have these big revelations, and you think they might go out and use them."

"That's not the case?" said Alice.

"Not really. They become obsessed with the muse instead. She unlocks something in them, and they believe that it was only possible with her help, so they essentially worship her. We've had to get ahead of a few cults forming around it. The art coming out of those sessions… it's all about *her*. It's meta garbage." She paused in her rant to take a sip of her drink and found it empty. Dan slid a fresh one her way. She took the first sip, then continued. "We're working on it. A small group of us are in charge of brainstorming tweaks in the touchstone's approach. We found one poem the other week that compared the muse to a sunset and then compared the sunset to a sunrise. It was a big day for us, seeing a line of verse that didn't include the muse. Granted, 'a sunset with the promise of a sunrise' isn't exactly sensational, but it's something. It could even be profitable if we packaged it the right way and marketed it to the right people."

"Ya know," said Alice, "Susy here is a poet. Quite a good one, too." Vel glared at her. "I bet if she could listen in on one of the touchstone's meetings, she'd have some great feedback to give."

Phoebe grinned greedily at Vel. "Really?"

"Yes," Vel replied through gritted teeth.

"She's taught workshops and everything," Alice added. "Her specialty is erotic poems."

Phoebe bounced in her chair. *"Really?"*

Vel balled her hands into fists beneath the table. "Yes. That's right."

"What are the odds?" Phoebe rubbed her palms together. "Erotic poetry is a top seller in our other marketplaces. If you could help the touchstone inspire this entire planet to create erotic art…" A visible chill ran through her, and she shook it out through her arms. "Come on." She slid off her stool and steadied herself on the table once her feet hit the ground. "I'll take you there right now. If I'm the one responsible for figuring this out, maybe the Depot will let me retire and spend the rest of my days on a party planet. Anywhere but here. Place is absolutely crawling with artists." She led them farther up the hill, winding through the crumbling streets, where crews in jumpsuits had roped off various buildings and struggled, mostly in vain, to add some basic structural integrity after the fact.

Alice caught more snippets of conversation from passersby:

"You don't have to read it to know it's bad. I can already tell you it's typical mainstream trash…"

"The member on that statue was totally unrealistic. No creature has a member that big!"

"Braindead woman wants to alienate half the solar system by depicting black holes as dangerous? Fine! See if I read any of her work again…"

Alice reached the end of the line for the muse before she realized what she was looking at. It twisted around the block, and Phoebe led them along it until they passed the door to enter the muse's studio. Instead of heading inside there, they went around the back and paused at a door with a large *Employees Only* sign. Phoebe knocked. "It's Phoebe. I might've found a solution! Let me—"

The door swung open, and a Bacc'joon glared at them with glassy eyes. Thankfully, it was a female, so the pants of its jumpsuit were only filled with legs. "Who are they?"

Alice, Dan, Vel, and Caid stayed a few paces behind Phoebe, waiting patiently for the invite.

"They're the solution!" Phoebe exclaimed.

"Are you drunk?"

"Corex Jon, you're not listening to me."

The Bacc'joon held her ground. "You're drunk."

Alice waited for Phoebe to plead her case further, but the Bacc'nali did something else instead.

She kicked Corex Jon in the face.

The Bacc'joon went down with a squeak and was out like a light.

Cringing, Dan asked, "Was that completely necessary?"

"No. But I'm sick of her judgment. Why's she judging me when her people massacred mine?"

Vel shrugged. "Fair point. Shall we?"

They stepped over Corex Jon's legs as they entered the poorly lit employees-only hallway.

"There's a meeting room this way. We're technically on our lunch break, but a few of the other jumpsuits might be back already. I'll tell them about the erotic poetry thing and see if *they're* smart enough to recognize a solution when it kicks them in the teeth."

As they followed her, Caid leaned toward Alice and said, "You know I would never want to be a source of unnecessary doubt for you, but I don't see where this is going, and I'm worried this might blow up the minute Vel is asked to recite erotic poetry."

Alice feigned insult. "You don't think Susy has a sensual side to her that's capable of erotic verse?"

"Please don't twist my words. But also, no, I don't think she has any access to that side of her being at this point on her inward journey."

"Don't worry. This'll work out."

"And what does working out mean to you?"

"It means"—she lowered her voice to a whisper—"we're gonna kidnap the touchstone."

"And then what?" said Caid.

"And then… And then… And then we'll take her back to the ship and peace out."

"And then?"

She held up her open palm between them. "Stop it. You know I can't think that far ahead."

When they entered the meeting room, two beings were already there. One was playing on a handheld device, eyes glued to it, and the other was eating a sandwich while staring blankly at the wall.

"Quintaer! Flibabang!"

Both snapped out of their stupors and stared wide-eyed at Phoebe.

"I might have a solution!"

The one who'd been playing on the device, and appeared to be mostly invertebrate, said, "Who are they?" He sounded like he was speaking through a mouthful of gelatin, but the words were easy enough to understand. "I don't see Depot patches."

"They're not Depot. But she"—she pointed to Vel—"is an *erotic poet*." Phoebe held up her hands like "ta-dah!" and waited.

The one who'd been eating a sandwich, and appeared mostly Homo sapiens except for the long trunk in the middle of his face, said, "Are you drunk?"

"Does that even matter? Think about it! We have someone who knows how to create real, marketable art. She's even taught workshops. Who better to help us train the touchstone?"

The mostly invertebrate grunted. "Nah, you'll just make the art they produce about the muse erotic. No one wants that."

"We don't know until we try. Imagine if this works! What do we have to lose?"

The one eating the sandwich turned to Vel and said, "Let's hear it, then."

Vel knew this moment had been coming since the first second Alice bullshitted about it. The multiverse wasn't ambivalent, after all. It had a sick sense of humor, and anyone who didn't see that wasn't paying attention. And so, Vel had remained mostly silent on their journey from the bar to the meeting room, trying her very best to think of a few lines of erotic poetry.

She'd failed. She hadn't gotten within ten feet of her own erotic impulses since she had a little too much to drink and probably some drugs on Bacc'nalia. Mustering up lines that sounded anything but stilted proved impossible.

Have I ever read a poem? she wondered.

She couldn't recall a time.

And now everyone was staring at her, waiting.

But one person was staring at her the hardest. She turned toward that laser beam and met Alice's eyes.

Alice, the captain Vel never asked for. More proof of the multiverse's sick sense of humor. Vel had killed people with her bare hands, played a crucial part in a galactic war much bigger than herself, and won awards and wild acclaim for it. She was a hero in her parallel universe. There might even be poetry about *her*, for all she knew!

Yet here she was, being forced to conjure sexy words out of thin air. The indignity.

Alice was mouthing something.

Hello? Allow?

When Alice tapped her ear, it all came together.

Vel whirled on her heels, putting her back to the room. To everyone else, it might've looked like an appropriately dramatic flourish. For Vel, it gave her the opportunity to whisper what she needed.

"Sounds dirty, Big Susy," came the voice in her ear.

And so it was that Supersymmetry Machiavelli, three-time winner of the Crab Nebula's title of Bloodthirsty Renegade, began reciting some of the dirtiest poetry that had ever been uttered in that particular galaxy.

"His length throbbing, rising like the swollen tides, he thrusts inside the slickness, pincers clawing skin, teeth meeting exoskeleton..."

Alice hugged herself tightly, biting her lip to hold back the giggles while the Depot workers gaped. Partially, the giddiness was from hearing those words leave Vel's mouth, but no small portion of it was owed to the fact that Alice, despite her aversion to planning, had been nearly prophetic in her one demand from the Alliance. If this worked, none of it would've been possible without Allura's deviance.

Vel's recitation of Allura's deep-coded fantasies came to an abrupt halt when the man who'd been eating the sandwich jumped to his feet, his trunk sticking straight out from his face, and shouted, "I can't take it anymore! I'm so horny!" before darting from the meeting room.

For her part, Vel hadn't been paying much attention to the content of the poetry as she focused on repeating whatever lines Allura fed to her. Only as she watched the man sprinting past her and out of the room did she realize she'd done a good enough job. Or rather, Allura had.

The mostly invertebrate shook his wobbly head and blinked away the fog of passion. "We've gotta get her in to see the touchstone right away." He jiggled his tentacles. "I'll notify you when she's finished with her current appointment."

Once he was gone, Phoebe turned to the group. "I don't know where you four came from or why, but you're making me believe in a benevolent multiverse."

Vel kept her mouth shut on that matter.

Rolling her shoulders back, Alice said, "Phew! Everyone okay? Dan, you all good after that?"

At some point during the recitation, the Pangolian's nervous system had maxed out and thrown him into a freeze state.

"Dan!" Alice snapped in front of his face, and he blinked. And then he started shaking. "Shit, jitters right now?"

"No," Caid said, stepping forward. "This feels totally different. I think his nervous system is completing the stress cycle by shaking. It's a prey response."

"Was it really that intense?" asked Vel.

Alice lowered Dan safely to the ground where he could

complete his reset. "Susy, I don't even know if I can look at you the same. And I mean that as a compliment."

Dan's shaking subsided, but a lethargy hung heavy on his shoulders, and his eyelids drooped conspicuously.

When the call came through on the intercom that the touchstone was on her break, Alice and Vel lifted Dan to his feet, and the four of them followed Phoebe out of the meeting room.

"Through here," the Bacc'nali said, pushing open a door and holding it for the guests to enter.

Alice stepped inside and paused. "Oh damn, this is wild."

Vel was the next in and paused beside Alice. "The erotic poetry wouldn't feel out of place here, at least."

Alice gently touched Vel's wrist. "Let's cool it with that for a while, Susy. At least until Dan can gets a booster in him."

The room was decorated like a palace brothel, but instead of a large bed, there was a pedestal at the center. Around the ceiling hung cloths of rich colors, some sheer, some heavy and textured like crushed velvet. Only the perimeter of the room was properly lit, leaving the pedestal and the figure on it obscured by layers of shadows.

The mostly invertebrate stood by the pedestal and waved them in. "This is them," he said to the figure.

"Don't worry," whispered Phoebe, "the touchstone isn't dangerous."

As Alice stepped closer, the touchstone turned to face her, and while a few things became clear, most things became less clear and downright confusing as Alice recognized this face immediately.

"Well, hot damn," she breathed.

CHAPTER
TWENTY-ONE

"What a pleasant surprise!" said the touchstone, hopping down from her pedestal and approaching the crew with open arms. Each knew that this was a trained gesture, not an actual invitation for a hug.

Liz Windsor didn't give hugs.

And yet there she went, wrapping her arms tightly around Alice. "I missed you."

Alice patted their former Depot liaison a few times on the back until the disconcerting hug ended, and as Liz Windsor proceeded down the line, offering hugs no one could refuse, except Caid, who still returned an air hug, nobody could quite articulate what they were thinking.

Mostly, what they were thinking was stuff like: *The fuck?* And: *How is this even possible?* And: *What are the odds?* And: *The fuck? How is this even possible? What are the odds?*

But it's exceedingly difficult for most intelligent life forms to verbalize the thing they are screaming inside, and so it was Liz Windsor who enjoyed the first words. "I never expected to see any of you again after you defected from the Depot and joined the Alliance."

"They what?" spat Phoebe.

"Don't worry about it, dear," said Liz Windsor. "You're in no danger." She stared at the group. "What are the odds? Improbable, certainly!"

"But they're traitors," the Bacc'nali protested. "Depot policy is to kill all traitors."

Liz Windsor reached out and patted Phoebe on the sleeve of her jumpsuit. "There's still time for that. No need to hurry. My goodness, we're so far away from anyone who cares that by the time the signal reaches them with this new development, we might all be dead." She turned to her former employees. "Come, let's have some tea and catch up. It's quite nice here. Much better than that concrete bunker I lived in on Blerg VFP69. No offense."

Alice held up her hands. "None taken. I didn't realize you lived there."

Liz Windsor offered a smooth smile. "Yes. It was like being in prison every day, a sentence that I thought would never end. But here I am! Funny how the multiverse works."

Phoebe was sent to fetch tea with a wink from Liz Windsor, who led Alice, Vel, Dan, and Caid over to a small, comfortable sitting area, not too unlike the lounge where they'd congregated at Depot Headquarters beneath the office supply store.

Caid opted to sit cross-legged on the floor by the low table, as Alice, Dan, and Vel settled on a velvet sofa across from Liz Windsor's wing-back chair.

"I apologize for the stunned staring," said Caid. "I'm so pleasantly surprised to see you."

"Yes, we're old friends, aren't we? You and I go way back." The reason why they went way back—they'd survived a lot of failed missions and outlived the crews on each—went unspoken.

"How are you here?" Vel said. "This doesn't make sense."

"It's extremely unlikely," Liz Windsor conceded.

Vel scrunched up her nose. "No, I get that. I'm sick of that, in fact. But how did you come to be here? And how come you aren't having us killed on the spot?"

Liz Windsor gaped and pressed a hand to her heart, appearing scandalized. "Miss Machiavelli, is that how you view me? A cold-blooded killer? I haven't ordered you to be killed yet because I like you. All of you. I considered you my friends before you left."

"And where's Doug?" Vel asked.

"Oh, he's dead. Yes, I had to decommission him. Depot's orders."

"He wasn't your friend?"

"Not at all. Couldn't stand him. Frankly, I missed Mark."

"Don't you mean Mike?" Alice asked.

"Hmm," said Liz Windsor, "maybe. Regardless, I'm here now. I worked hard enough that I finally earned myself a promotion! Once I hired on the new DeepService Team One, I was sent here on a new mission."

Phoebe appeared with a tray of tea and set it on the low table.

Liz Windsor grinned at her. "That will be all. You can leave."

Phoebe looked like she was about to speak, but miraculously held her tongue and stumbled out of the room.

As the touchstone stirred into her drink what Alice presumed was honey, she said, "The Depot has taken a serious interest in the arts recently. That's why I'm here. They believed that, due to my track record of loyalty and my deep understanding of interpersonal communication, I was the perfect representative to bring on as a muse, to wrangle the tortured psyches of these artists and lead them to fruitful pursuits."

"Huh," said Alice. "I would've assumed this was a demotion. Punishment for your crew taking off on you and joining the Alliance."

"No, no, this is a step up."

Alice forced a smile. "Whatever you say."

"Alas," Liz Windsor continued, "we have not seen the success so far that we had hoped for." She leaned forward. "Between us, I'm beginning to doubt that art and commerce are completely compatible." She cleared her throat. "But really! How are the four of you? What brings you out here to Putterpantsia?"

Alice looked to the others to see who wanted to start. Dan avoided her gaze. Caid appeared lost in a blissful haze at seeing his old friend.

Vel, though. Trusty Vel. She was more than happy to speak up, and Alice was more than happy to watch her do it.

"We're here because the Depot is drilling at the edge of the universe. It's reckless. It's homicidal. It's the act of a megalomaniac on too many boosters. The odds of their finding a neighboring universe with the same dimensions as ours are low to begin with. Then you multiply that by the thousands of drilling sites—and those are just the ones we know about—and the odds of this working out in any way other than the erasure of the entire multiverse and the arrow of time along which we all exist is so low as to be essentially zero."

"Well, yes," said Liz Windsor. "The drilling is rather unfortunate. But I asked how you ended up *here*."

"The managers on Location," Vel replied. "One of them gave us these coordinates and told us to find the touchstone. We had no idea it was you."

Liz Windsor's brows rose like marionettes on a string. "Oh, that *is* interesting. Which manager on Location? I'll have to have them eliminated, of course."

"Then we're definitely not telling you," said Alice. "Liz Windsor, do you know why we were directed to you for this cause?"

The liaison took a long sip of her tea then shrugged. "A diversion, perhaps? Send you in the wrong direction? I don't know why you would trust a manager to support you on your subversion, frankly."

"No," said Vel, shaking her head firmly. "No. I won't accept that this has been a waste of our time. This can't be a dead end."

Dan finally spoke up. "Are you going to report us? Are you going to kill us?"

"I have no desire to kill you myself," replied Liz Windsor. "As for reporting you, I should. Technically my chip is recording all of this and sending it back to the Depot."

Alice felt her stomach sink, and the distinct and unproductive urge to sprint out of the room and back to the ship threatened to overtake her. Instead, she gripped the couch cushion beneath her and held herself in place.

Liz Windsor licked her lips. "However, the Depot is overwhelmed by the amount of information it collects every second. The artificial intelligences that sort through the data for relevancy have been threatening to strike. There's simply too much to do, and their servers are constantly on the verge of collapse. So, were I to *forget* to add an urgency marker to the data of our conversation, there's a strong likelihood that it would never come to the attention of those who would care."

Dan and Alice locked eyes. Something was happening with Liz Windsor. Something totally unexpected.

Alice placed a palm on the table in front of the liaison. "We need your help. Everyone needs your help. I think you know who runs the Depot. I think you've always known. I reckon that's why the manager sent us to you."

She waited for confirmation, but the response she received was a strange one, and she didn't know what to make of it.

Liz Windsor began tapping on her chest, thrumming her fingers in what appeared to be a random pattern. Then she abruptly stopped and bowed her head.

For a moment, Alice wondered if the woman had malfunctioned or decommissioned herself. Or maybe she was dead. Whichever one applied more to the iffy line between human and machine that Liz Windsor walked.

But then she raised her head again and said, "I've disconnected from the Depot."

"Huh?" said Alice.

"Just now?" asked Dan.

"For how long?" asked Vel.

"It's temporary—five minutes, currently—but I can prolong it if necessary. Tell me what you need. Do it quickly and precisely."

"We need to speak with whoever you report to," Vel said, jumping in. "We have to go to the top. We don't want to overthrow the Depot, but we need to convince everyone who has a say in it to stop drilling. We need you to take us to them. Will you do it?"

Liz Windsor frowned. "It's not within my programming to move against the Depot."

"Please," said Alice. "We're begging you. There's no pretending this isn't happening. If there was a way to avoid this mess, you bet your ass I'd be all aboard that train. But there ain't. It's all or nothing. The Depot has us on a collision course with erasure, and for what? For the near-zero chance that they'll only drill into compatible universes and can expand their control? They're making this decision for all of us, Liz Windsor, and it's not fair. It's not right. This is the only multiverse we've got, and they're threatening to destroy it and all of its history. And for what? Greed? More money? Can they even spend all the money they already have?

"I miss my planet, Liz Windsor. Every time I think about how much I miss it, it feels like someone set off a ticking time bomb in my chest, and I gotta disarm it with distractions or it'll explode. I'll never get any of my Earth stuff back. It's all gone. That coffee shop I loved, the sun setting over the farm, my hound dog pawing—" She swallowed it down. "I'm all that's left to remember those little things. I regret leaving it, Liz Windsor. Goddammit, I regret ever leaving it! I've fucked up so bad, and it's led me here. So all that's left for me is make it right somehow. But I can't do that unless you help us. If you refuse, I—I don't know where else to go. I might as well help with the drilling myself, because the horror of waiting to be erased is too much. You're our last-ditch effort, friend. I never saw it coming, but out here in Jesus-less space, you're my only chance of salvation."

Liz Windsor's plastic expression gave away nothing.

And then she sniffled. "Dammit all! I fear I have more human left in me than I care to admit. Perhaps it's my time on this planet. Perhaps the artists have inspired the muse." She addressed Caid. "I'm sorry for not doing more. I still think about Djaar, Marifa, Svat'palnka, and Terry in quiet moments."

He placed his hands over his heart, and a shimmering tear appeared on his cheek. "Thank you for saying that."

"There was a time when I was fully human, back before my accident required that I change into what I am today. I think about her often. She's always felt like a different person, and one I missed, because she felt so distant. But now I'm wondering if she's still inside me. If I'm her." Liz Windsor set down her teacup and rolled her shoulders back, perking up. "I've just remembered her name! It was... Dawn." She laughed. "How wonderful. Her name— *My* name was Dawn." She inhaled deeply, and perhaps it was a trick of the light, but Alice thought she saw small lines appear at the corner of Liz Windsor's eyes as the woman smiled. "Yes, I'll take you where you need to go. We'll stop the drilling together, whatever it takes."

And then, one of the drilling stations struck through to a brand-new universe, and it was the most unlikely thing: the foreign universe had the exact same dimensions as ours, and so the multiverse didn't disappear, it grew.

The arrow of time went on, pointing unflinchingly toward—

Oops! Another drilling station broke through, and this universe had vastly different dimensions, so everything was erased like *poof!*

Although, thankfully, *that* did not happen in the reality we've been following.

In this reality, Alice heaved a sigh of relief and was the first, outside of Liz Windsor, to reach for her cup of tea.

"Ooop!" Liz Windsor slapped Alice's hand away. "No,

no. Don't drink that. I gave Phoebe the signal to poison your cups before we had this lovely conversation. One sip and you'll be dead. I would hate for you to die *now*, however, just as we're embarking upon such a grand adventure together!" She spread her arms wide. "Look at us! Everyone is back together again! I must say, this feels like a homecoming! For once, I'll be an *official* member of DeepService Team One." A sliver of a crease appeared between her brows as she frowned. "But no, I don't suppose we can call it that anymore." She looked around. "We'll need a proper name if we're to continue on as a crew."

Alice's gaze wrenched itself free from the poisoned cup, and she grinned wide-eyed at Liz Windsor. "That's what I've been saying! Getting anyone to agree on one is impossible, though." She glared at Vel.

"Ah, well, I've remembered something from my human days that might work," Liz Windsor began. "How about the Space Oddities?"

The others responded with a collective groan.

"Woof," said Alice. "I get it now, Susy. It sounds *super* lame when someone else comes up with it." She leaned across the table and patted Liz Windsor on the shoulder. "Keep your chin up, though. You tried, and that counts for something." Then she slapped her knees and stood. "No regrets. Now, let's go save the multiverse."

MORE ADVENTURES

Want to know when the next Alice Luck Space Adventures is available to read? Join my email list, and you'll be the first to know.

Sign up: www.hclairetaylor.com/hi

I'll also send you infrequent updates on life, funny stories, and bonus content. I don't do the spammy thing, don't worry. Join the fun. I dare you.

ABOUT H. CLAIRE TAYLOR

H. Claire Taylor is the author of the **Jessica Christ** comedy series about God's only begotten daughter; the **Kilhaven Police** series, which follows a rookie human cop getting his ass kicked in a city of paranormal beings; and the **Alice Luck Space Adventures**, one of which you've just read.

She lives in Austin, Texas, with her husband, John, who laughs at all her dumb jokes and is generally the love of her life.

Claire is also the owner of FFS Media, through which she publishes the books she writes under her four pen names.

instagram.com/claireorwhatevs
amazon.com/author/hclairetaylor
bookbub.com/authors/h-claire-taylor

BOOKS BY H. CLAIRE TAYLOR

The Alice Luck Space Adventures

Lucky Stars (Book 1)

Cluster Luck (Book 2)

Ship Out of Luck (Book 3)

Luck Off and Fly (Book 4)

The Jessica Christ Series

The Beginning (Book 1)

And It Was Good (Book 2)

It's a Miracle! (Book 3)

Nu Alpha Omega (Book 4)

It is Risen (Book 5)

In the Details (Book 6)

The End is Her (Book 7)

The Kilhaven Police series

Shift Work (Book 1)

Same Old Shift (Book 2)

Shift Out of Luck (Book 3)

Deep Shift (Book 4)

Wimbledon, Kentucky

See all at www.hclairetaylor.com

Find more books at www.ffs.media